Seven Wishes

A Story Collection

By

Jeff D. Brown

Others by Jeff D. Brown
Vampire War: Nemesis
Dead Time Book I

This book is a work of fiction. Names, characters, places, and incidents either are products of the author's imagination or are used fictitiously. Any resemblance to actual events, locales, or persons, living or dead, is entirely coincidental.

Copyright © 2016 by Jeff Brown

All right reserved, including the right to reproduce this book or portions thereof in any form whatsoever. For information contact Jeff Brown c/o My Lair Workshop, 106 North St. Enterprise, MS 39330.
ISBN:

First publication October 2016

TABLE OF CONTENTS

1. Eternity……………………………………………………….5
2. In The Storm……………………………………………...22
3. Junkman……………………………………………………41
4. Parallels…………………………………………………...49
5. Retaliation………………………………………………...69
6. The Escape………………………………………………...85
7. Chatawa…………………………………………………130

ETERNITY

Eternity is a story about obsession, indecision, and choices. The three sometimes work together to create a situation that can be both good and bad. I've attempted to make this one kind or morally vague. Sometimes the right decision, the one that you think will give you everything you want, will end up giving you something you never bargained for.

The inspiration for this story actually goes all the way back to my first semester at the University of Southern Mississippi. As a music major, I was required to attend an assembly of all music majors that ended up determining locations for a particular class that we were all required to attend at the same time. Before that assembly began, I looked around for a familiar face and didn't see very many, but I did see this one girl that caught my eye. I never really got to know her, but that brief moment was enough to spark this story nearly thirty years later.

I looked up and there she was, walking toward the main classroom building. I was seated on a concrete bench beneath the lone massive oak tree at the front of the Markham Academy campus beside my girlfriend of the last two years, Stacy Harris. But my attention was drawn to Carly Beech when she walked onto campus that morning in early October.

I didn't know what it was that I found so fascinating about Carly. She was a short girl, thin to the point of looking almost emaciated, with a thick mass of chestnut brown dreadlocks perched atop her head and flowed down to almost the middle of her back. Her full lips looked a little too large for her small, narrow face and her chocolate brown eyes seemed just a little too large. The small gold band set in the left corner of her lower lip and the multiple ear-rings added to her mystique. But she dressed oddly, wearing ankle-length dressed and skirts with well-worn sandals.

She was something of a loner. She had transferred from the Marsdale Public School system just a week into the semester and rumor had it that she had been kicked out of the public school for multiple dress code violations and multiple incidents of leaving campus without permission. That was a lot for the first week of the school year.

Still, I couldn't help staring at her. She seemed so vulnerable and isolated. I didn't think she had any friends at the school. She never talked to anyone and didn't really say much in class. I had two classes with her, but I always sat near the front, trying to be a good student, while she sat at the back and appeared to be completely disinterested in the educational process. Stacy had yet to notice my preoccupation with the new girl. She was too interested in spreading gossip about others and relaying her supposed inside information to her best friend, Karen Bryce.

Stacy was an attractive girl, considered the best-looking girl on campus, and I should've felt fortunate to have spent two years dating her, but it just wasn't the ideal relationship I'd expected. She was of average height, standing about five and a half feet tall, with a long shock of straight brown hair and eyes the color of emeralds. She was a cheerleader and kept her body toned and tanned. She didn't like tanning beds or tan lines. She spent nearly every day during the summer working on her tan in her secluded and practically impenetrable back yard, completely nude. She'd even included me in one of those tanning sessions, but I just didn't get the whole idea of lying in the sun with nothing to do for hours on end. I did enjoy being so close to her naked body, but that was the height of the experience for me and it wasn't repeated.

I watched Carly until she was out of sight and inside the classroom building. Still, my thoughts were on her as I turned back to the conversation going on between Stacy and Karen. Karen, an inch shorter than Stacy with slightly shorter and slightly darker hair, pale brown eyes, and a soft, pale body, sat on another bench facing Stacy. They both leaned forward as if conspiring or trading secrets. Stacy's boyfriend, Tony Miller, sat beside her. He was a football player, as was I, but we'd never been friends. I played offense and he played defense. The two units rarely had contact off the field.

The girls were discussing yet another girl and her shortcomings.

Elaine Jenkins was their target of the day. Of course, they wouldn't physically do anything to her, but they would talk about her incessantly and break down every detail of her life that they knew about. I did my best to ignore them and was happy to leave them when the bell rang to begin the school day a moment later.

We parted amicably, as we always did, and with a light kiss. It had been a long time since we'd shared a real kiss and I'd begun to think the relationship was nearing its end. Still, I liked to watch her walk away. There was something about the tight jeans she always wore and the way she walked that I just had to watch. But it wasn't enough to keep a relationship going. I walked quickly to my first class. I wasn't in a real hurry to start working on an essay, but I wanted to be in the vicinity of Carly Beech.

I entered the classroom and she was already there, sitting in the back of the room in the corner closest to the window. She was staring out that window and actually glanced in my direction as I entered the room and walked to my seat. Our eyes met and a thin smile played across her large, pale lips. I returned the smile, feeling slightly embarrassed, but I made it to my seat without tripping over anything or falling on my face.

I took my seat, dropping my dark blue backpack to the floor beside me, and leaned over to pull out a notebook and pen I knew I would need for the class. As I did, I risked a glance at Carly. She was staring at me and that small smile remained on her face. I looked at her for the few seconds while I fumbled in my bag for the items I needed.

She had crossed her legs and the hem of her dress had pulled up, revealing the pale flesh of her lower legs and just a hint of knee. I looked up to her face and noticed that the smile was just one aspect of the hungry expression that clouded her features. She wanted something, but I didn't know what it was. I definitely didn't think it was me.

Then she switched legs, crossing her left over her right. As she moved, I swore I caught just a hint of darkness between her legs. When I looked at her face again, she just nodded and returned her gaze to the window. I shook my head and sat up, preparing myself for the writing assignment I knew was coming.

I felt completely drained at the end of that class and wasn't paying attention as I walked for the door. As usual, I was the last one to leave. I took my time packing my bag and I knew every day that procrastination was due to my reluctance to go to my next class. I didn't like doing all the work in English, but I hated Math.

But as I stood up and started for the door I realized I was not alone in the room as I'd thought. Carly was waiting beside the door with her few books clasped to her chest. The teacher had the next period off and had already departed for the teacher's lounge. That left me alone in the room with Carly.

As I started for the door, Carly took a step toward me and finally stopped me near the center of the room.

She looked up at me and said, "I need you to do something for me."

"What's that?" I asked.

She smiled lightly, one side of her mouth curling up as she said, "I saw how you looked at me before class."

I nodded slowly and said nothing. I let her continue.

"I need you to meet me tonight," she said, her voice dropping in volume. "There's something I have to show you."

"What?" I frowned.

She shook her head and said, "I can't tell you. I have to show you. Meet me behind the old dairy on Highway Thirty tonight at ten."

"I don't know," I said and shrugged.

She placed a hand on my chest and smiled again, "You won't be disappointed. Trust me."

She looked at me a second longer then her hand dropped away, she turned around, and walked quickly out of the room. I remained in place a few more seconds until it struck me that I was running later than usual for Math class.

I survived the remainder of the morning, but I couldn't get Carly off my mind. Even at lunch, sitting at a table with Stacy leaning against me and her soft breast pressing against my arm, my thoughts drifted to Carly and our brief conversation. I was intrigued by what she'd said and what she'd asked me to do. The more I thought about it, the more determined I grew to meet her behind that old dairy farm and see what she had to show me.

Carly was in my History class after lunch, but she didn't say anything to me and she wasn't waiting after the bell rang to end the period. She did smile again, but we were seated on opposite sides of the room and there was no repetition of the possible flash she'd shown me that morning.

I didn't see her after school, but I hadn't expected to. I had football practice and I didn't know her class schedule. I didn't know where she ended the day. I looked for her briefly as I made my way from the Political Science class to the field house, but I didn't see her. I finished practice and went home. I'd take a shower after practice and didn't really need another. I didn't have any homework that night and nothing to do for a few hours, if I was indeed going to meet Carly. I tried reading a book, but it couldn't hold my interest. I finally turned on the TV in my bedroom and settled on an old movie channel and watched that mindlessly until dinner was ready at seven. I ate and returned to my room, thinking more and more about Carly and what she wanted to show me.

I decided I would meet her. Curiosity got the better of me. I wanted to know what she had in mind and I had no way of contacting her or finding her before the appointed time. So, I waited.

I left my house about nine-thirty. The drive from my house to the old dairy only took about ten minutes, but I definitely didn't want to be late. I was always early for everything, something my parents had drilled into me practically since birth. And I was just too anxious to see her again.

I reached the old dairy on Highway Thirty with fifteen minutes to spare. I parked in the shadow of a massive tree near the building that had at one time been the milking barn and climbed out of the car, leaving the door unlocked. For some reason, I thought I might have to get in the car and start it quickly. I pocketed the keys and began walking around the deserted farm. There were several buildings there of varying size and shape. I had no idea what any of them had been used for other than the milking barn. And I only knew that because my dad had told me the first time we'd driven past the place. I'd expressed no interest in learning more about the place and he hadn't been inclined to tell me more.

After a few minutes, bored of looking at old, deserted buildings, I remembered that Carly wanted to meet behind the farm. I hadn't thought to bring a flashlight and there wasn't much moonlight that night. It was dark and it took me a few minutes to reach the back of the farm. There was a large field there, the pasture where cattle had at one time grazed, with a line of trees on the other side of it and a heavy wooden fence separating the buildings from the pasture.

Standing beside a narrow gap in the fence was Carly Beech.

She leaned against a post and stared at me until I noticed her presence and walked toward her. She stood up and waited until I was facing her before she said, "Come with me."

She took my hand in hers and led me across the pasture.

She didn't say anything as we walked slowly toward the tree line. Her grip on my hand was loose and comfortable, her hand soft and dry. I kept looking at her, risking only quick glances to keep my attention focused on the ground ahead of me. I didn't want to stumble and fall. I didn't want to embarrass myself in front of her. She still wore the ankle-length dress she'd worn to school that day, or at least one very similar to it. It had been a sky blue dress with light colored flowers scattered on its surface and this one seemed dark with lighter patches. I could be sure, but it didn't really matter. We were together and one our way for her to reveal what she wanted to show me.

We reached the tree line a few moments later and entered on a narrow trail I hadn't known was there. Carly apparently knew about it and walked confidently along it. Still, the pace was slow and the woods were darker than the field. I had a hard time making out even the shapes of the trees lining the path, but Carly seemed to have no problem.

After several long minutes, I began to see something ahead of us that looked like a glow. I frowned, thinking that something was wrong. We were going away from town and there shouldn't have been any lights that deep in the woods. As we neared it, I began to think that someone had set a fire, but I soon realized that we were approaching a clearing and there was a campfire of sorts at its center.

Carly stopped at the edge of the tee line, just before entering the clearing. She looked at me and said softly, her voice barely above a whisper, "Stay here until I tell you it's time. You'll understand and you'll enjoy it."

I nodded and she stepped a little closer. She reached up and placed her hand on the back of my neck. She pulled me closer, leaned in, and kissed me.

At first, I was taken slightly aback by the presence of the golden hoop in her lip, but that didn't last long. I quickly felt the passion in the kiss, a passion I hadn't felt with Stacy in a long time. I knew then, at that moment, that my relationship with Stacy was definitely over. I really had no designs on Carly, but there had to be someone out there I was more compatible with than Stacy. Then after a few seconds, she pulled me even closer, her left hand at my waist, and her tongue slipped into my mouth. I felt her small, firm breasts pressing against my chest and I knew she wasn't wearing a bra. That excited me a little more and I didn't want the kiss to end, but it did after just a moment. She pulled away and let me go. I gasped, more from the intensity of the kiss than the breathing I hadn't been doing.

"Wait here," she said. "Trust me."

I nodded and she turned away, walking out of the woods and into the clearing.

She was silhouetted by the blazing fire less than thirty feet away and I watched as she walked slowly toward it. Her small hands reached up and began working at the front of her dress. She took only a few steps more and the dress fell to the ground. She stepped out of it and kept walking, now wearing only her sandals. I couldn't see any details, but just the idea of her walking naked toward the fire aroused me like I'd never been aroused before.

As she neared the fire, I saw movement beyond it. There was just a brief blur behind the flames that became a solid figure as the much taller person beyond it stepped into view.

The firelight revealed the form of my Science teacher, Nancy Chambers, and she was naked as well. My eyes grew wide in the dark. I hadn't expected that.

Miss Chambers was one of those teachers that all the kids talked about and frequently fantasized about, myself included. I'd watched her in class and had wondered on more than one occasion what she would look like naked. Now I knew and it was everything I'd imagined and more.

Carly stopped a couple of feet from the fire and removed her sandals, tossing them haphazardly to the side. The two naked females then walked to each other, embraced, and kissed. I definitely hadn't expected that. My hormones almost got the better of me then. I almost rushed out into the clearing to see what would happen, but I restrained myself.

Carly and Miss Chambers, after breaking their embrace, stood facing each other and appeared to be talking, but I couldn't hear what they were saying.

A few minutes later, a third girl approached. She entered the clearing from the far side and walked toward them. I shifted position slightly, moving quietly, to get a better look at the new arrival. As she stepped into the firelight, I recognized her.

Janet Lakin was a tall, lean blond with large breasts and sea blue eyes. I'd never taken much notice of her at school. She was younger than me and ran in different circles. I'd just never paid much attention. Now, she had my undivided attention as she began quickly undressing and soon stood naked with the other two.

She first embraced and kissed Miss Chambers then moved to Carly. They seemed to hold the kiss a little longer and it made me wonder. Still, I remained in place and watched.

When Carly and Janet broke their kiss, Carly said something to her, then to Miss Chambers, and started walking toward me. I stood my ground and waited until she entered the woods before I moved at all.

She stopped in front of me and said, "Come in. It's time. But first, take off your clothes."

"What?" I asked, confused.

"Take off your clothes," she said. "It won't work if you're dressed."

Before I could do anything, Carly reached for my shirt and started pulling it over my head. I helped her with that then, as I was unbuckling my belt, she knelt in front of me and untied my shoes. In mere moments, I stood naked before her. She took my left hand with her right then ran her left hand slowly between my legs. She gave my erection a gentle squeeze then led me into the clearing.

I was embarrassed and excited at the same time. I had never been anything close to an exhibitionist and I tried never to expose myself, even unintentionally. I didn't want anyone, especially attractive females, to see me completely naked. But it wasn't quite as bad as I'd imagined it to be. There were no crude remarks or laughter. The other two just looked at me and smiled. As I grew closer to them, I could better make out the details of their bodies and I enjoyed that.

But as I neared, Miss Chambers looked to her right briefly then looked at me and said, "Perfect timing. The others are here and they've brought our guest of honor."

I frowned at that. I'd been thinking that the night and the meeting had been for me. As Miss Chambers turned away to greet the new arrivals, Carly looked at me and said, "Erik, this may be a shock, but we want you to be one of us. You have more potential than any male I've ever heard of. I saw that the first day of school. But there's just one thing you have to do to join us."

"What's that?" I asked. I seemed to be asking the same questions over and over.

She then took a step back and held her arms wide, fully exposing herself in the light of the fire. She smiled and said, "If you do this one little thing, this will be yours for as long as we live."

She pointed toward the other women and said, "We'll all be yours."

It was weird. I'd been thinking about a new relationship, but not three or four. I just wanted that one girl that could keep me excited and interested.

Then Carly lowered her arms and started around the fire.

"They're here," she said. "And the biggest surprise is with them."

I turned and followed her around the fire with Janet falling in step beside her.

Two more girls were approaching and they carried a third between them. The third girl was naked and had a cloth concealing her face. I couldn't make out details in the dark, but they moved closer and I recognized the girl on either side of the blindfolded one. They were Alicia Morgan and Elaine Jenkins.

As they stepped into the light, I looked at the naked body between them and thought I recognized it, but I wasn't sure until she was within ten feet.

The naked girl was Stacy.

It had been a long time since I'd seen her naked, but she looked every bit as fantastic in the dim light of the fire as she had in the blazing sun of a summer afternoon.

Before I could say or do anything, Alicia and Elaine lowered Stacy to the ground then began removing their clothes. Within moments, they stood there naked as the rest of us. They took turns embracing and kissing the other women then finally turned their attention to me, all of them. They took turns kissing and fondling me. I really didn't mind that, but I wanted to know what they intended to do with Stacy.

Carly was the last of them. She kissed me, embraced me, fondled me, and finally guided my hand between her legs. She kept her hand on mine, keeping it there for quite a while.

When she finally broke the kiss, I held onto her, grabbed her arms and leaned closer to her.

"What's going on, Carly?" I asked. "Why is she here?"

Carly smiled, "It's all part of the ritual. We need a sacrifice to bring you into the fold."

"The fold? Sacrifice? What the hell?"

She took my hand and led me away from Stacy as the others moved toward her. We walked a few feet past the fire and she said, "Erik, we found the secret to immortality. It's in the communion of souls. The sacrifice of a single life, no matter how insignificant, is enough to grant immortality to one special person. Right now, that person is you."

"You want me to kill Stacy so I can live forever? That's bullshit."

"No," Carly shook her head. "Do you know how old I am?"

I shrugged, "I'd guess about seventeen."

She shook her head, "I'm ninety-four, Erik. Janet is the young one. She's only sixty-one. Alicia is eighty-five and Elaine is seventy."

I didn't believe it. I shook my head and said, "And what about Miss Chambers?"

Carly chuckled, "Nancy is a hundred and twenty-three. She's the one that saw the potential in all of us. And it's been a long time since we've brought in a new member. But Nancy says you have more potential than the rest of us combined. Just imagine what you could do if you knew you'd live forever."

I did think about it. I'd never really considered my mortality before that night. I knew that everyone lived and died, some longer than others, but I hadn't thought I would die anytime soon. But I did have something of a fascination with the future. I'd read a large number of science fiction novels and stories and I'd always wondered what life would be like after my death, what technology would show up. The idea that I could live forever sank in and wouldn't go away. But it would mean the death of Stacy, the girl I'd spent almost all of my spare time with for the previous two years. It meant taking another life and I wasn't sure I was ready for that. I looked at Carly and she apparently saw something in my expression.

She smiled and said, "It's not that difficult, Erik. And there's more to it than just living forever. I could explain everything, but that was would take all night. We need to do this before midnight."

The truth was that I just didn't care about Stacy anymore. I hadn't actually liked her since a couple of months after we'd started dating. She'd actually grown rather annoying. I'd wanted to get away from her for a long time, but I hadn't been able to bring myself to actually pulling the trigger and ending the relationship. I was ready to do that. I just wasn't sure I was ready to kill her.

I looked over at the others. They had Stacy staked out on the ground, her legs spread and her knees were slightly raised. The blindfold remained in place.

Carly moved in front of me and said, "Now's the time, Erik."

I looked at Stacy again and realized that I wanted immortality more than I cared about her life.

"Fine," I said hoarsely. "Let's do it."

She took my hand and we walked back to the others. They stood in a semicircle around Stacy. Carly positioned me at Stacy's feet and I looked down at her. She left me and took a position between Janet and Elaine. Nancy walked over to me holding a small dagger in her hands. She stopped in front of me and held the dagger out. I reached for it, but she pulled it back.

She looked me in the eye and said, "You must have intercourse with her and you must plunge the dagger into her heart at the moment of climax. Then kiss her and hold it until she breathes her last breath into you."

I nodded and she gave me the dagger.

As she moved back to her place in the semicircle, I lowered myself to my knees and crawled between Stacy's legs. As I moved into position, Nancy reached down and quickly removed Stacy's blindfold. She opened her eyes and looked at me as I penetrated her. She gasped and I began thrusting. My mind wasn't on the dagger or what I would be doing in a few moments. It was on the sensation and the pending release.

Stacy glared at me, unable to say anything. I was glad of that. I didn't want to try explaining what I was doing. She wasn't capable of understanding. I just continued doing what I was doing while the five naked women watched in anticipation.

I felt the release coming and glanced up at Carly. She smiled at me and nodded slowly. I looked at Stacy again. Her eyes were closed as her orgasm began to reach its peak. I matched her intensity and raised the dagger into position. Stacy gasped and I knew she had reached climax. That triggered my own and, as I shot my load into her, I plunged the dagger into her heart. I immediately leaned forward and planted my lips on hers. Her body bucked beneath me and I struggled to keep my mouth over hers. Finally, after a couple of long minutes, she breathed her last breath into my mouth.

I sat up and didn't feel any different. I pulled out of the dead body and looked up at the others. Carly walked over to me, knelt beside me, and wrapped her arms around my shoulders. I think the look of shock on my face made her want to comfort me. The feel of her bare flesh didn't mean much to me at the moment.

Nancy walked closer to Stacy's body and stared at it for a moment. She leaned over and pulled the dagger free. She then walked over to me as Carly said softly, "There's just one more thing."

Nancy crouched in front of me and looked me in the eye, "This is your proof."

And she plunged the dagger into my heart. I screamed.

Carly just laughed.

Nancy pulled the dagger out and I looked down at the blood that covered my torso.

The pain faded. The wound healed.

I looked up at Nancy and she said, "Now, you are immortal."

Then Carly kissed me and all was right with the world again.

IN THE STORM

In The Storm is just another take on vampires. I've come up with several ideas for vampires and this is possibly the most recent version. It's also another version of the old clichés. "Don't judge a book by its cover." "Everything isn't always as it seems." "There's more than meets the eye." The basis of this story came to me while riding out Hurricane Isaac a few years ago in an old, crappy trailer near the Mississippi Gulf Coast. Of course, there were no vampires and no girls wandering in to take off their clothes. But there was a lot of wind and a lot of rain. Still, I never lost electricity and I survived the storm, obviously.

Riding out a hurricane in a thirty-five-year-old trailer less than a hundred miles from the Gulf of Mexico was not exactly my idea of fun, especially when you're barely seventeen, a high school senior, without transportation, and a hundred percent on your own.

Of course, I knew the storm was coming days ahead of time and so did my parents, but there had been no real choice to be made there. My father was a long haul trucker and he'd been sent on a cross-country run two days before the storm's anticipated arrival. He wouldn't be back for well over a week. My mother was a nurse and worked at a hospital on the coast. She'd been unable to find a full-time position at our local hospital and kept the one she had. It paid more and was better suited to her specialty – pediatric nursing. So, she had been called in with the first team for the emergency preparedness response to the hurricane. That meant she had gone to the hospital eight hours before the storm was expected to make landfall and she would work a seventy-two hour shift before being relieved for twenty-four. Then she would be on for another seventy-two hours before finally being permitted to return home. Still, that meant another eight hours or so of rest before she could drive back to our small town.

Shortly after her departure, I'd begun making preparations of my own. She'd left me with two hundred dollars, an exorbitant amount, for supplies and necessities. I think she counted on the fact that the only business within walking distance was Joe's Quick Mart barely a hundred yards from the entrance to the trailer park. She didn't think I would find enough there to spend the entire two hundred on and would have some left when she finally returned home.

I wasn't intentionally trying to spend all of her money, but I was going to be prepared for the storm at all costs. I walked to the store just a couple of minutes after her battered old car had pulled out of the driveway and turned toward the coast. It took me only a few minutes to walk there and I could already see the clouds rolling in as the hurricane's feeder bands were approaching. I didn't think it would be long before the rain and wind started.

Inside Joe's, I began gathering what I thought I would need. I grabbed a loaf of bread, two jars of peanut butter, a few bags of chips, some cookies, bottled water, soft drinks, candy bars, and the few canned vegetables on their shelves, dusty cans that had almost reached their expiration dates. I added in a large flashlight and enough batteries to last until the end of time.

As I walked back to the trailer with several large bags in hand, I thought that I may need gas for our generator. The electricity was sure to go out at some point during the storm and I wanted enough in reserve to keep power to at least the refrigerator and microwave for the duration of the storm. I hadn't thought to bring the two red plastic cans with me and I was somewhat glad of that as I trudged back to the trailer with the supplies in hand. The cans would've been too much to carry with all that stuff.

I returned to the trailer and unloaded my purchases, placing the water and soft drinks in the refrigerator in the southeastern corner of the trailer, then walked back to the store and bought ten gallons of gas. Those two containers, filled, weighed at least twice as much as all the other stuff and I had a hard time getting back to the trailer. I walked slower and had to stop a couple of times.

I should mention that I'm definitely not the most physically active person on the planet. I'd always been rather thin with little muscle tone no matter how much I worked out and tried to eat right. Besides, my pursuits were more of the intellectual variety than the physical. I spent a majority of my time at my computer working on some silly little story or playing a ridiculously difficult video game.

I finally made it back to the trailer, just in time to almost be run over by the Hispanic family, the Ortega family, pulling quickly away from their trailer in their bright red SUV. The wife and mother, Raquel, waved almost sadly as the vehicle shot past me and, with the cans in my hands, I could do nothing other than to nod.

I went to the end of the trailer that faced the west. It had the widest open in the metal skirting around the base of the trailer. The generator was there, hooked up and ready to go. I placed the two gas cans in there beside it then crawled under the trailer. I hadn't thought to bring the flashlight with me after buying it, but there was enough light to let me see what I was doing as I crawled beneath the structure and checked the ties that held the trailer to the earth. There were six spots where the frame of the trailer was attached to the ground with thick steel chain. Six holes had been dug, supposedly five feet deep, and filled with concrete. A large eye bolt had been set in the concrete and the chains were attached to the bolt with a locking clip. I checked each of them to make sure the rings were still attached and that the chains were secure. I was satisfied that they were and I backed out of the crawlspace. I'd never liked going under there and had been a little more apprehensive than usual that day. The coming storm had undoubtedly sent a plethora of snakes, spiders, and bugs into that small bit of refuge and I just hoped that nothing too poisonous attacked me. I received a few insect bites, nothing too large, and I was glad that the spiders and snakes had left me alone.

  I went back inside and started securing things inside the trailer. I was satisfied that the trailer's frame was secured to the ground, but I wasn't quite so sure that the trailer itself was firmly attached to the frame. We had a lot of small items stashed around the trailer and I spent a good half hour rounding them up and stuffing them in an old cardboard box I'd found in my parents' closet. From there, I cleaned up their room, getting things out of the way and putting some masking tape on the windows in case they shattered. Then I went to my room.

  It was the smaller of the two bedrooms in the trailer and barely large enough to hold all of my stuff. My bed was tiny and shoved in a corner with a small stand beside it. One corner held a small desk for my computer and a built-in desk of sorts just inside the door was where my TV and DVD player rested. My various games, discs, movies, and books were scattered around the room. I didn't really feel like picking them all up at the time and just made sure my computer and TV were secure. I made sure the small window was locked and taped before closing the door and returning to the living room.

I took a minute to make sure everything there was secure, which it was, before going into the kitchen. I shook my head as I entered and knew that there was no hope for the items in there. The refrigerator wasn't quite full, but there were enough things in it to negate the possibility of transferring them all to a cooler for the duration of the storm. Then there were the dishes, all stack neatly and perfectly arranged in the cabinets over the sink and stove. I had nowhere to put them to keep them from being thrown all over the place. I decided to just leave the kitchen items where they were. I did put up the remainder of the things I'd bought at Joe's.

I was putting the last two items, the two jars of peanut butter, in one of the cabinets when the storm finally arrived.

It started with a heavy gust of wind, but it couldn't have been much over twenty miles per hour. Still, it was enough to rattle that crappy old trailer. I wasn't surprised, but it did give me a bit of a start. I shook my head at my own insecurities and decided I should take care of everything possible before the storm reached its peak. I went to the bathroom then took a quick shower.

Wearing only a pair of jeans and with a towel wrapped around my shoulders, I returned to the living room and turned on the TV. It was already set on the weather channel and I just had to sit down for a minute and watch the updates. Of course, the national media had little to say about Mississippi. All their attention was focused on Louisiana. I wanted to know more about what was headed my way, but for that I had to change the channel to one of the stations broadcasting from the coast. I picked up the remote and changed the channel.

I watched for a while, watching the coverage of the storm surge as it inundated the coastal areas and the flooding began. I knew that I was far enough away from the coast that the flooding due to the storm surge wouldn't really affect me. Finally, I had enough of the growing disaster and went to my room to finish dressing.

There was no mirror in my bedroom and I had to go into the small bathroom beside it to comb my hair. It was a lackluster light brown and hung to my shoulders, covering my ears. I stared into the mirror for a long moment and compared my slate gray eyes to the mass of clouds outside. I saw the storm in my gaze and wondered which would break first.

I wasn't quite afraid of the storm or its results. I hated living in that trailer and almost hoped that it blew away. Of course, that meant I would be in it at the time and I wasn't quite ready to move on to the next life just yet. There were certain things I wanted to accomplish first.

When the stories started repeating, I moved away from the TV, walking around the trailer, and looked out the windows to see what was going on.

The wind was hitting me from the northeast, so I went into the kitchen and looked out the small window over the sink. I had to lean forward, resting my arms on the edge of the metal sink, and looked out through the falling rain. The wind wasn't too much just yet, but the rain was heavy and reduced visibility greatly. Still, I was able to see the trailer across from mine, an even older one. The middle-aged couple that lived there had already evacuated and the trailer stood empty with only one of their vehicles parked beside it, a black pickup. They'd taken the wife's SUV since it would hold their belongings without them being soaked by the rainfall.

Beyond that trailer and the empty spaces on either side of it, I could see the line of newer trailers that faced the other side of the horseshoe shaped path through the park. There was a line of small, widely spaced trees separating the two lines of trailers and they were already bending wildly in the wind. I didn't think they were ready to snap or topple, but they were definitely moving. I couldn't tell if any of the people on the other side had evacuated. I didn't know many of them, tending to stay on my side of the park, and I couldn't see their yards clearly.

I moved away from that window and to the one to my right, beside the refrigerator. It was a larger window and I'd already opened the blinds to give me a better view of the narrow asphalt drive that curved around from the entrance drive and continued past my trailer to the large green dumpster about a hundred yards away. As I looked toward the entrance, barely visible past the three trailers and two cabins along the path, I saw one last family finally getting out. They were hastily loading things into a massive pickup, the kids climbing into the back of the cab. I watched until they finally locked the door of their large cabin, climbed in the truck, and drove quickly out of the park. I shook my head and walked away from the window.

I went to the back of the trailer next, into my parents' bedroom. The largest window was there, facing the opposite direction of the small kitchen window. It afforded a view of the wide drainage ditch about twenty feet behind the trailer and the line of trees that served to identify the park's property line. The water in the ditch was already a couple of feet higher than normal and the current was flowing north. Seeing that, I knew that it wouldn't overflow anytime soon. There was a pump at the back of the property that fed the ditch into the city's main sewage system and it had been turned on. I didn't waste a lot of time there and returned to the living room.

I sat down in the recliner in one corner of the room and stared at the TV in the opposite corner. I picked up the remote from the coffee table just to my right and adjusted the volume. The wind began to howl and the rain pounded the roof, making it difficult to hear the TV.

The weather and the stories hadn't changed and I soon fell asleep despite the mild vibrations running through the trailer with the wind striking it.

I didn't wake up until something struck the side of the trailer and rattled the entire structure. My eyes snapped open and I sat up in the recliner, kicking the footrest down until it locked in place. I stood up and looked around quickly. I then hurried through the trailer looking for any sign of damage. The electricity was still on and I found no damage and no leaks. I walked back to the main entrance. The back door, just outside the rear bedroom, had a bad latch and normally wouldn't stay closed. My dad had boarded it shut over a year earlier and it remained that way.

I opened the front door and was immediately assaulted with a heavy dose of water, blowing rain. I shook it out of my eyes and looked around. I didn't see anything that could have struck the trailer and I assumed it had to have been a falling limb somewhere on the other side. I wasn't going out to look for it. I quickly closed the door and returned to the recliner.

It was dark outside and I'd obviously slept longer than I'd intended. I was hungry and went into the kitchen to find something to eat. I settled on a couple of peanut butter and jelly sandwiches. I ate them and wondered what to do next. The TV was still on, still airing stories about the storm and I was growing a little tired of them, though I still wanted to know what was headed my way.

While I was making the sandwiches on the small table beside the large window, I looked up. Lightning flashed and briefly illuminated the entire area in a stark blue-white light. My eyes were briefly dazzled, but I thought I saw something out there, something that shouldn't have been there at the height of the storm. I quickly finished the sandwich and took a bite as I stepped closer to the window and peered out.

I couldn't see anything. The kitchen light cast a reflection and wouldn't let me see what was outside. I stepped back and flipped the switch down, turning off the light, and returned to the window. The ambient light coming from the living room still made it slightly difficult, but I could see enough to tell that there was someone outside, moving slowly toward me, being buffeted harshly by the heavy wind. Whoever it was had long hair, plastered to their head and upper body, and was fairly slim. Then lightning flashed again and I knew who was headed toward me.

Keri Reston lived in the last trailer in the line. She was a year younger than me and a student at the same high school. And she was also the most beautiful girl I'd ever seen. Of course, I hardly knew her and wasn't quite sure she even knew my name. But she looked to be in trouble at that moment and I wasn't going to leave her out there at the mercy of the Hurricane Gretchen.

I dropped the remains of the sandwich on the paper plate I'd left on the table and practically ran to the front door. In the five steps it took me to reach the door, the idea of putting myself in danger ran through my mind. I pushed it out just as quickly, convincing my worried mind that I was practically invincible since I was on my way to help someone else.

I opened the flimsy door and the wind ripped it immediately out of my hand, slamming it back against the outer wall of the trailer. I wasn't concerned with the door at the moment. I ran out and hurried down the rickety wooden steps that led to the small wooden porch, my hands slipping on the rain-slick metal hand rail. At the bottom of the steps, my tennis shoe-clad feet splashed into a puddle of water maybe four inches deep. The cold water immediately soaked through the cloth shoes and socks.

I took one step toward the next trailer, toward Keri, and the wind slapped me in the face like a giant hand. I was staggered back a step. I caught myself, braced myself for another strong gust, and pushed forward. I pushed forward, grinding my teeth together as I struggled against the wind, and reached the next trailer, a vacant one, about forty feet from my door. I grabbed onto it and pulled myself to the corner. There, I found a better grip and pulled myself up right. I squinted against the driving rain and looked around the corner.

Keri was still trying to walk toward me. I guess she knew that I was still there and that everyone else had evacuated. I guess I seemed like her only hope. She had her arms wrapped around her and staggered slowly forward, being pushed to her left with each step. Her jeans were soaked and clung to her legs like a second skin. She was barefoot and her head was bowed. I didn't think she saw me.

I called out to her as loudly as I could, but I could tell that the wind stole my voice as it left my mouth. I took a deep breath to steel myself for the wind and was rewarded with a mouthful of water going down my throat. I coughed briefly and spit it out the best I could then moved around the corner.

Keri still didn't see me. Her eyes were still focused on the ground in front of her. I took a couple of steps and leaned forward as I reached the tongue of the trailer's frame, still attached. I placed a hand on it to steady myself and stepped around it. I called out again and Keri finally looked up. I held out a hand to her and she moved a little more quickly. She was about thirty feet away and the look of relief on her face was almost heartbreaking. I wasn't much and neither was my trailer, but it was apparently better than what Keri had. I took a couple of tentative steps toward her, still holding out my hand, and she ran to me. At the last second, just before our fingers touched, a gust of wind pushed her to the side. I lunged toward her and wrapped my hand around her wrist. In almost the same motion, surprising myself, I reached back and grabbed the edge of the tongue, a bar of steel protruding nearly four feet from the edge of the trailer. That piece of metal saved us. I pulled her to me then, as the wind subsided a bit, I turned around and pulled her toward my trailer. I held onto her hand and pulled her up the steps to the door. The steps shuddered with each step, threatening to collapse, but we made it to the porch and inside. The door had remained open and a good amount of rainwater had been blown into the trailer. My wet shoes slipped on the wet tile floor and I almost fell, but my left hand on the frame of the door kept me more or less upright. Keri came in just behind me and I turned around to close the door.

I leaned out and grabbed the knob. It was loose in my hand, as it always was, but the few screws holding it in place remained attached and I pulled the door closed, fighting the wind. As it closed, I turned around and looked at Keri.

She stood just a few feet inside the door, water dripping from her jeans and somewhat tattered light blue t-shirt. The wetness of her clothing had them clinging to her body and I actually took a couple of seconds to admire her form. It was fantastic, but I didn't linger on it. She wasn't there for me to hit on her. She was there because she needed help.

Once the door was closed, I walked toward her and asked, "Are you okay?"

She looked at me, her big blue eyes almost pleading. They were ringed with read as if she'd been crying recently. I attributed it to the wind and rain being slammed into her face as she'd made her way toward my trailer.

She shook her head and said, "No. They're out there."

"Who?" I asked, frowning. "Who's out there?"

"Them," she said and looked around almost frantically.

Before I could ask for more details, she hurried into the kitchen and closed the blinds over the window. Her wide eyes and almost spastic motions made me think that she was definitely afraid of something. I just didn't know what it was.

I followed her into the kitchen and stopped behind her as she closed the blinds then turned around.

"What's going on?" I asked. "You can trust me. I just want to help."

She looked at me for a second, almost as if she didn't recognize me, then shook her head again and said, "You won't understand. I shouldn't have come here."

I held my hands out wide, "Where else could you go? There's no one else here."

She pushed past me and stormed back into the living room, trailing water. I shook my head and followed.

She stopped beside the door, her right hand reaching for the knob. I leaned toward her, extending a hand, and said, "You can't go back out there. You'll never make it."

She paused and looked at me. She cocked her head to the side and said, "You really just want to help me, don't you?"

I nodded slowly, "I couldn't let you stay out there and get killed by this storm. But who's out there? Is someone after you?"

She nodded slowly, "Yeah. He's sort of an ex-boyfriend, I guess. His name's Tristan Oliver."

I'd never heard that name before. There were three high schools in the area and I guessed he went to one of the other ones, or he was in college. Keri seemed like the kind of girl that would go for an older guy. She was too much for a high school kid.

"It's okay," I said. "He can't get to you in this storm. You're safe."

"No," she shook her head. "He can go anywhere he wants. He'll come for me."

"Why is he after you?"

She stared at me for a second, her brow furrowing slightly in thought as she considered her answer.

"I broke up with him," she finally said and took a step closer to me. "He didn't want that and he said he'd make me pay."

I still didn't understand and she obviously didn't want to say anything else about it. So, I let it go and changed the subject. I took a step toward her and said, "Give me a minute. I'll see if I can find you some dry clothes."

She nodded and her shoulders sagged, relaxing just a little. I walked toward my bedroom and she followed. I hadn't expected that. I thought she would wait in the living room while I found something and it would give me time to change discreetly as well. But she followed and we entered my tiny bedroom.

There was barely enough room for us both to stand in there, but I acted like it was no big deal. I went to my closet and opened the door. I looked around and found a pair of sweat pants and a t-shirt that would probably be a little large on her, but looked close enough. I pulled those out and handed them to her then turned back to the closet to find clothes for me. I quickly found another pair of jeans and a t-shirt along with dry underwear. I didn't have anything close to underwear that would work for her and she would just have to make do.

I turned around to tell her that the bathroom was next door and she could change there, but she was already removing her clothes. She pulled the t-shirt over her head slowly, the wet cloth sticking to her skin, and I turned away after catching just a glimpse of her now practically see-through bra.

I nervously looked back in the closet and pulled out a neatly folded towel. I shook it out and held it toward her as I said, "This might help."

She moved closer and took the towel.

"Thanks," she said, but didn't move away, just resumed removing her clothes.

I heard the wet slapping sound as her shirt hit the floor then a slight grunt from her and I assumed she was reaching behind her to unclasp her bra. I didn't look, but I imagined.

"It's okay," she said as something else hit the floor. "I don't mind being seen."

I wanted to look, but I just couldn't. It didn't seem right. But I debated it for a moment.

With the door blocking my view, I knew I was out of her line of sight as well. I hastily pulled my wet t-shirt off and ran my hands through my hair. I pulled out another towel and dried my chest and hair a bit, while kicking off my wet tennis shoes, before putting on the other shirt.

As I did, she said, "Suit yourself."

I took that to mean that she was standing there completely naked and was ready to start dressing. I resisted the temptation and let her dress while I quickly peeled off my pants and underwear, dried myself, and dressed just as quickly.

I took a chance then, sort of giving in to the temptation, and stepped back. I turned toward Keri just as she pulled the t-shirt down and into place. I didn't see anything other than her well-toned abs. She then looked at me and shrugged, "Your loss."

I was surprised at the sudden change in her demeanor. She had seemed completely frightened and nervous just a few moments earlier and now seemed more of the stuck up girl I'd sort of assumed her to be. She ran a hand through her hair and it fell into place almost perfectly. I never understood how girls could do that.

Then we went back into the living room and she took a seat on the sofa. I sat in the recliner and looked at the TV. Keri looked at me. She didn't say anything for a few moments, just sat there staring at me. It made me feel a little uncomfortable.

"He's going to come for me," she said after several long, tense moments.

I looked at her and said, "I don't think he can go anywhere in this storm."

She shook her head slowly, "You don't know Tristan."

She fell silent then and sat back, her gaze going to the TV. I stared at her a moment longer then returned my attention to the TV. I watched for just a few moments and didn't really want to see any more of what was happening in other places. I was more concerned with my situation. I stood up and walked into the kitchen. The light remained off and I walked to the window over the sink. I looked out and was surprised that I was able to see anything. I couldn't see it clearly, but I could see the trailer and truck across the narrow road through the park. I watched as the wind blew sheets of water from the roof, knowing that the water was replaced almost immediately by the heavy rain.

Just then, the wind picked up again. I saw the trees, their silhouettes actually, bend farther than they'd bent before. One of them, beyond the perimeter of the trailer park, snapped off nearly twenty feet above the ground. Then, the trailer across from me began to lift off the ground. I remained motionless, unable to do or say anything, just watched as it slowly rose off the ground. The screech of metal, tin and aluminum, rending filled the air along with the snapping sound of chains breaking. The rectangular shape of the trailer distorted, bending and collapsing at the corners as the far corner lifted off the ground and it seemed to hang there for just a second before finally flipping over with a huge crashing sound and it rolled over onto its roof.

"Oh, my God," I said softly and watched as it settled then looked back to where it had been. There was someone standing there. It looked like a rather large guy standing just past the corner of the space where the trailer had been resting. He was just standing there, looking at me. I knew he was too far away for me to see any details of his features and it was so dark that I could barely see his shape, but I swore I could see his eyes, glowing darkly.

He took a step toward me and I swore that he had seen me and was heading toward me. I wanted to move back and go hide in a corner. He scared me that much. But I stayed there and watched him. He moved slowly, methodically, stalking toward me, and he didn't seem to be affected by the wind. Sure, his clothing and long hair blew in the wind, but he walked as if it didn't exist.

I almost jumped out of my skin when I felt a hand on my shoulder. Keri had walked up beside me and placed a hand on my shoulder. I looked at her, but she didn't look at me. Her attention was focused out the window.

But she only looked for a second. She stood up and looked at me then said, "That's Tristan."

I looked out the window again, just as he stopped beside the pickup. He crouched slightly and reached under it with his right hand, never taking his gaze from me. He casually stood up and the side of the pickup rose with him. Then, with a flick of his arm, looking like nothing more than raising his hand to run his fingers through his hair, the truck flipped over. I flinched as the sound of the crumpling metal reached me and Keri stepped back.

I stood up and looked at her. She folded her arms across her chest and said, "You can't stop him."

I didn't know what to do. If he really was that strong, there was no way I could do anything to stop him, to keep him away from Keri. Hell, all he had to do was flip my trailer like he'd done the other one and we'd both be dead. He wouldn't have to worry about us fighting back.

I didn't have long to worry about him. Less than a minute later, he was at my door. He didn't knock and I couldn't remember if I'd locked the door or not. It didn't matter; he just ripped the door from its frame and tossed it casually over his shoulder.

Then he entered the trailer.

Keri was quickly at my side. Well, sort of behind me. She wrapped both of her arms around my left and peered over my left shoulder. I felt the weight of her body against me and she felt cold. I guessed that the rain had taken its toll and she hadn't yet warmed up.

Tristan entered the room and, though he was only about an inch or so taller than me, he seemed to loom over me. I felt like I was standing in the shadow of a skyscraper. He was dressed in all black, as I'd expected, topped with a black leather jacket. His hair, even longer than mine, was darker than his clothing. His eyes still seemed to glow, but it was a dark light behind them. His skin was pale, looking as if he'd been in the storm for a while. Keri had looked like that when I'd found her, but she seemed to have started warming up.

Tristan took two steps into the trailer, rain blowing in behind him, and stopped just a few feet from where I stood with Keri behind me. He stood there for a second with his arms dangling loosely at his sides, his hands open. Mine were clenched into fists, ready to defend this girl I barely knew. I glared at him for everything I was worth, but it didn't faze him at all.

He took another step closer and completely ignored me, acting as if I didn't exist. He looked at Keri and said, "You're coming with me."

"No," she said and I felt her head shake. "I can do this."

His face finally showed some sign of emotion, but just a bit. The left side of his upper lip curled up slightly as he said, "This is not right, Keri. You're not ready."

"I think I am," she said.

I wondered what they were talking about. She'd told me that he was a psycho ex-boyfriend, but he was inhumanly strong. There had to be something more going on.

"You were not supposed to come here," Tristan said, his voice thin and cold.

"This is my time," she said, her voice growing somewhat angry, somewhat desperate. "You can't stop me."

"I can," he said. "I'm stronger than you."

"I don't care," she said and Tristan snarled, leaning slightly forward.

As his lips parted, I saw that there was something wrong with his teeth. I'd felt like an intruder in an argument between two people I didn't know. When I saw his teeth, the overly long incisors, I knew it was more than that. I was way out of my league. I leaned away from Keri, trying to extract my arm from hers, but she held on and I couldn't move.

He took a step toward us and Keri made her move.

She spun me around, grasped my shoulders with both hands, and leaned me slightly backward. I felt like a rag doll in her grasp. I looked at her and saw that her red-tinged eyes had taken on a darker red quality. Her full lips parted then and her own fangs had extended. She suddenly went from the most beautiful girl in the world to the ugliest.

From the corner of my eye, I saw Tristan take another step toward us, but there was nothing I could do. Keri, however, did something. Her head snapped forward and her fangs plunged into my neck. I felt a moment of exquisite pain followed by an intense, comforting warmth. My eyes closed and my consciousness slipped away.

I died. It took a moment for that to sink in when I opened my eyes.

But Keri was there to explain everything.

I was lying in a bed, but it wasn't mine and I didn't know where it was. Keri sat beside me on the bed. Tristan stood behind her. He didn't look quite as menacing as he had in the trailer.

"You're one of us now, Matt," she said with a smile on her face.

Then she shrugged and said, "Well, you're not quite there yet, but you're close."

Tristan then stepped around her and looked at me. He smirked and said, "I guess you're tougher than I gave you credit for being. Not everyone can accept the Change, but you've come through the first part. The next is easier."

"What do you mean?" I asked, looking from Tristan to Keri. "What's going on?"

Keri leaned closer, kissed me gently on the cheek, and said, "Well, Matt Harper, you are now a vampire."

JUNKMAN

Junkman is kind of a throwback to my teenage years. Back then, in the late 70s and early 80s, I was obsessed with science fiction. I saw every movie that came to the theater in my small town, regardless of how bad it actually was, and I read every book I could find in the public library. There was no bookstore in the town at the time and the library was my only option for a while. I was obsessed with the works of Robert A. Heinlein, Arthur C. Clarke, Ray Bradbury, Frank Herbert, Harlan Ellison, Phillip K. Dick, Ben Bova, and a number of others. I read for entertainment back then, but I eventually realized that it had been research.

The junkman's ship hovered twenty meters above the dusty, barren soil of a small, gray planetoid's surface. It was a relatively small celestial body, but one that had not yet been explored or exploited. He knew that a full survey team from the Interstellar Alliance would arrive with a month to begin searching for any available resources. If so, the IA would mine the planetoid for every ounce of usable material. The junkman just wanted to get what he could before that happened.

He had discovered the planetoid quite by accident while traveling through that solar system to reach the nearest hyperspace corridor, on the other side of the system. He'd flown past it with his scanners searching for anything and had located a few items on the surface of that planetoid that had looked promising. These items indicated a previous visit from some ancient race and he was certain they would bring a decent price on the open market. He just had to get them before the IA survey team arrived.

In a way, he was thankful for impending arrival of the survey team. Upon the announcement of the survey, the IA had shifted the entrance to the hyperspace corridor closer to the planetoid, less than eight hundred thousand kilometers away from its previous position at the edge of the solar system. That saved him two weeks of travel and a small fortune in fuel costs. He chose not to land on the surface of the planetoid at all. He wanted the IA survey team to find no sign of his presence. They had ways of tracking even the most minute details to the source and he didn't want to be discovered in the position of the relics he was certain would soon be in his possession. It did cost fuel to keep the ship stationary above the surface, but that cost was minimal compared to the travel through the entire solar system he would've had before the shifting of the corridor.

It would have been more efficient for him to move his main vehicle, the Galbor, from place to place as he discovered items worth removing, but he trusted his eyesight and the instruments on his smaller craft, a sub-orbital crane, than those aboard the larger, older Galbor. It was also less likely to be noticed by any advance probe the IA might send. With the larger ship parked in the shadow of a massive, craggy mountain, it was effectively hidden.

The planetoid held no breathable atmosphere and SOC was an open cockpit vehicle. He had planned for that and had purchased a newer model personal atmosphere regeneration unit just for that expedition. He'd checked it out prior to departure from his base of operations and verified that it would function as needed.

Leaving the lower bay doors of the Galbor open, he left in the SOC for his first target, nearly thirty kilometers away.

He took the SOC no closer than six meters above the surface, again to conceal his presence. The powerful lifters on the small craft would disrupt the dusty soil and leave a trail that the IA could follow and identify.

On the slow ride to the initial target, the junkman had time to think and he let his mind wander. As he often did, he thought about his past.

He had begun his adult life as an IA conscript, drafted into service near the beginning of the Fallorian War. Initially, along with thousands of other conscripts, he had been trained to be an infantry solder. The training had been minimal, confusing, and rushed. The higher powers had been in a rush to throw a massive number of bodies against an equally equipped foe without concern for the welfare of those soldiers. Most didn't survive the initial conflict, but the junkman had.

During the retreat from the home world of Falloria, the junkman had somehow ended up at the controls of a landing craft and had successfully piloted it out of the atmosphere and back to the home ship. After that, he'd been given instruction as a pilot and had served ten years in the IA fleet as a pilot, beginning as a fighter pilot and concluding as a capital ship pilot.

Then the war had ended and he'd been forcibly retired. He learned that his home had been destroyed and all the salary that he'd sent there to help his family had been confiscated by the IA upon his retirement. That left him just enough funds to leave his home planet forever. He worked various jobs as pilots, mostly for black market operations, and made enough money to finally buy the Galbor. That was when he began his salvage operations.

He started working for a group of other salvage men until he saved enough to strike out on his own. Since then, he'd earned a meager living, just enough to keep himself fairly well supplied and capable of going where he could find work.

He'd just chanced upon the planetoid and saw something there. It didn't appear to be that much, but definitely worth the trip once the hyperspace corridor entrance had been moved.

He reached the first location twenty minutes after departing the Galbor and hovered over the first item. It was a large platform of sorts, definitely not something natural. It looked nothing like anything around it. The thick octagonal platform, over a meter in height, rested on four spindly legs that ended in flat disc supports. The top looked scorched, as if something had ignited there at some point. His first thought was that it had been some sort of sacrificial altar. It was mostly white, but was lined with crinkled gold. The junkman assumed it would be worth quite a bit.

He positioned the SOC over the platform and lowered the crane cable. He then leapt from the cockpit of the SOC and allowed the light gravity of the planetoid to slowly draw him to the top of the platform. He moved around it carefully and found places to attach his lines. As he did so, he looked around the space surrounding the platform. The area was littered with strange footprints. The overall shape of the prints was oval with evenly spaced ridges between them. He didn't understand them. He'd never seen anything like them before.

Once his lines were secure, he climbed up the central cable to the cockpit of the SOC and activated the crane. The platform was heavier than it looked and the crane's winch motor strained to lift the item. But once it was off the surface, it became easier to transport. He returned slowly to the Galbor and unloaded the platform. He closed the outer bay doors and pressurized the hold. Then he detached the platform from the SOC then maneuvered it into a storage position using four portable lifters, one under each of the strange discs. That took quite a while and he decided to cease work for the day. He retired to his cabin and went to sleep. Several hours later, he woke up, ate a small meal, and returned to work.

He was at the second site just over an hour later and this one looked a little more challenging. There was not only a platform at this location; there was also a vehicle. The platform was nearly identical to the first, but the vehicle piqued his interest.

It wasn't quite as large as a standard vehicle had been on his home world, but its method of motivation seemed positively ancient. Rather than lifters, it had odd metal wheels. They were hollow and the mesh surface made that apparent.

The junkman didn't take long appreciating it. The vehicle was no more than salvage material at the moment. He took it back to the Galbor then returned for the platform.

While attaching the cables to the platform, he looked around the area again. There were more of the odd footprints, but this time he saw something nearby that he had to check out. A glint of pale sunlight glinted off a tiny bit of metal, something unique to that planetoid, and he had to see what it was. After lifting the platform with the crane, the junkman relocated the SOC to the spot where he'd seen the metal.

He first took a spare line from the cabinet behind the cockpit and attached it to the SOC. He dropped it over the side then made his descent.

It was a tiny piece of metal, oddly shaped, and was attached to a thick square of white cloth. He picked it up and returned to the SOC. He wondered about that piece of metal as he slowly made his way back to the Galbor.

He was over halfway there when he noticed the arrival of the IA probe. It just appeared over the horizon and he only had moments before it recognized his presence. He quickly located a dark area in a depression several meters to his right. He steered the SOC there and lowered it into the depression, hiding it completely in the shadows. He set it down and shut down all the power. Once that was done, he turned on a device attached to his belt.

The probe would be scanning for power sources and life signs. The Galbor was protected by the mountain. The probe wouldn't be able to distinguish its power source from the radiant energy of the mountain. The SOC was a different story. Without power, it was undetectable, but his life signs would be clearly visible. The device on his belt masked his life signs, but it would only work for several minutes.

He sat and waited until he was fairly certain the probe had passed him by. He then reactivated the power and lifted off. The lifters blew up a small cloud of dust, but that couldn't be helped. He then pushed it as hard as he could toward the Galbor. He knew his salvage mission was over and just hoped he could get back to the Galbor before the probe completed another orbit.

As he traveled, he scanned the horizon for the probe and occasionally looked behind him to see if it had recognized anything and was following him. He saw no sign of it and soon reached the Galbor.

He docked with the larger ship and didn't bother trying to lock down the platform still attached to the SOC. He just made sure it was properly docked and he began the process of preparing for departure.

He knew that the probe would be alerted as soon as he powered up the main drive, but he hoped that it was be far enough away that he could depart without being recognized.

As the reactor power built, he risked a look out of the darkness. Using the active lifters, he had the ship rise several meters. He quickly scanned the area and saw no sign of the probe. He heaved a sigh of relief and completed the power up process.

As he was engaging the engines, an alarm sounded, alerting him to the fact that the probe had noticed him and was nearing striking distance. With a barely whispered curse, he activated the main drive unit and the Galbor began its ascent, gradually building momentum.

As he rose above the height of the mountain, he opened the main view port and saw the probe rapidly approaching. Its roughly cylindrical shape had changed. It now had the appearance of a larger flat surface at its tip. The junkman knew that it had opened its weapons bays and was ready to engage.

He worked furiously at the controls, trying to push the engines to gain speed more rapidly than they were designed to, and happened to glance out the view port as he swung the nose of the ship in the general direction of the hyperspace corridor entrance.

He paused for just a second as he saw the remains of a nearby planet, large pieces of rock still occupying the orbital area where it had resided for uncounted millennia. He could see a myriad of small pieces floating along the massive chunks of planet and some of them looked like bodies. If he'd been able to stay longer, he may have investigated.

As it was, he set the appropriate trajectory and blasted away from the deserted moon.

PARALLELS

Parallels somewhat addresses a topic that I've often found intriguing. Are there actually parallel dimensions, alternate timelines, other planes of existence? If so, how would it work. The possibility of time travel has also been of great interest. So, I figured I'd combine the two and see what happened.

But I didn't want to use one of the more widely used forms of time travel. I didn't want some sort of box or vehicle to house the time machine. I wanted it to be something different and definitely with limitations. But, with most time travel stories, there are consequences.

I always liked knowing how things worked, even time.

I dedicated my life to the study of time and how it worked. Yeah, I'd been called a genius, brilliant, all those things that made me seem like something I really wasn't. I may have had the intellect, the education, and the creative mind that defined a genius, but I never claimed to be one. I did more research into time and how it worked than almost the entirety of the human race before me. Most people thought it was pure idealistic research, that I wanted to give to humanity an understanding of something that had, in some or other, baffled everyone on the planet at some time or other. The truth was that I had something a little more selfish in mind. I wanted to travel in time, go back to a very specific point, and change one little detail that I was sure would change everything.

I wouldn't physically travel back in time; only my consciousness would travel. After nearly thirty years of research and planning, that was the only way time travel could conceivably work. The laws of Physics stood in the way of true, physical time travel, but those laws weren't applicable to what I had in mind.

The process wasn't as complicated as you might think. It started with a fairly complex map of the brain. That was phase one of the research project. With the help of a team of neurologists and computer technicians, we accomplished that in just over five years. From there, I studied the map and located the points in the brain that remained constant. Some said I'd discovered the location of the human soul, but I don't think it's anything like that. I just found the points that delineated a particular brain from another. I found the mental equivalent of a fingerprint.

With that, the theory I'd had for a while began to take shape. With the help of particle acceleration theory, the theory stated that a temporal distortion could be created, but it would only last for a few seconds, at the moment of collision. Eight years of research there allowed me to replicate the process without attaching anything to one of those massive supercolliders that occupied as much space as some countries. I could do it in a room no larger than your average hospital room.

With the addition of the brain mapping process, the temporal distortion could be focused on a particular mind, a particular person. By fine tuning the frequency of the distortion effect, the distortion could be further focused to a specific date. The distortion was linked to the brain scan and would basically contact that person at an earlier date. From there, with two to three seconds of viability, the consciousness of the two entities could be transferred. The computer engineers that I'd brought in were the best in the world and they rose to the challenge. The transfer speed of that much data could be accomplished in just over a second.

There remained only one issue. The two brain patterns had to be in the same relative state for the transfer to take place. For instance, if we were both awake, the thoughts of both had to be focused in precisely the same direction. The person the present would have to be thinking about a melting scoop of vanilla ice cream at the precise moment that the person in the past was thinking the same thing. The only option that created a possibility was if both present and past persons were asleep and not yet in a dream state.

We tried a couple of times before figuring that out. In retrospect, I realized the concept should have been apparent from the beginning. I had been just too thrilled that the process was that far along. I'd expected at least another five to ten years of research and design before achieving any measure of success. Once we realized what the process was lacking, it took only a little more to be prepared for another test.

Of course, I was the test subject, over the protests of my assistant, Angela Parkland.

She was a short woman, perhaps ten years my junior, with jet black hair that hung in uneven strands to her shoulders. Her dark eyes were small and wide, separated by a small nose over thin lips and a slight under bite. She had a rather dark and sarcastic persona, but she was brilliant and the somewhat light-hearted opposite to my sullen intensity. She was far from being one of those "smile all the time" happy people, but her dark humor somehow seemed to fit the project nicely.

She was actually Dr. Angela Parkland, holding a degree in Physics as well as a medical degree. She was qualified to operate the medical machinery necessary for the process. I, on the other hand, was simply Dr. Paul Barnes, renegade theoretical Physicist, trying to put my theory into practice.

We entered the lab, a small room at the back of the science building at the university where we both worked, early on a Saturday morning in late October. I was forty-seven years old and wanted to be seventeen again, if only for a brief period.

I would go to sleep and wake up in my seventeen-year-old body. I would go through one entire day of high school again then return to sleep. When I slept, I would revert to the present and my aging body. And while I was in that younger body, my younger self would be in my older body. We had briefly considered the concept that the younger self would have to be awake when I was awake to ensure the successful return, but I did the math and proved that wouldn't be the case. Once the transfer was complete, the temporal distortion would dissipate and we would be separate entities. In truth, I could make the transfer permanent, but only by disconnecting the machinery and leaving my younger self to fend for himself thirty years in the future, at least to him. I couldn't do that to myself. My body would remain asleep for the duration of the experiment.

Angela and I spent a long time setting up and preparing the equipment. While she set up the transfer protocols, I calibrated the distortion. I had a very specific date in mind, one that I felt would change the outcome of my life.

I was forty-seven and still single. There was one incident in my past that I believed was the key to changing that fact, and hopefully only that fact. I believed that I had taken everything into consideration, but I was wrong.

We finally had everything ready to go shortly before eleven that morning. The frequency of the distortion was set to relocate me to a date less than two months before my high school graduation and two weeks before my eighteenth birthday. That was the day I believed would change my destiny.

The big issue still remaining was the retrieval process and when to initiate it. One theory held that time was not fluid, meaning that my older body would have to remain asleep for the duration of my waking experience in the past. Another theory held that time was fluid and Angela could begin the retrieval process almost immediately after my departure.

The final solution came rather easily once I sat down and thought about it. I set up the distortion device to scan the brain map of the past. It would do so every fifteen minutes for the duration of the experiment. Once the two patterns matched, the process would be reversed and we would both return to our proper bodies. All Angela had to do was initiate that process once the transfer was complete.

I changed into hospital scrubs and stretched out on the old hospital bed we'd brought in just for the transfer. Angela took her time and connected the leads from the distortion and brain mapping devices, making sure they were connected properly. It took a while, but time was something of which we had no shortage.

Once that was done, she administered an anesthetic and I soon found myself falling asleep. I closed my eyes and drifted away.

I woke up, opened my eyes, and experienced a moment of disorientation. I was no longer in the lab and no longer felt the innate aches and pains of my age. It took me a moment to realize that the experiment had worked, at least initially, and I was looking at the ceiling of the bedroom I'd occupied during high school. A smile slowly spread across my face as I realized that I could actually change the past and affect the future.

I sat up slowly, pushing back the heavy blanket that covered me. It was March and still rather cool outside. I'd practically forgotten that the old house had not been equipped with central air and heat. I was wearing a dark blue long-sleeved t-shirt and gray sweat pants with thick white socks.

I swung my legs over the side of the bed more energetically and happy about going to school than I ever had when that had been my present. When I stood up on the cold, tile floor, I took a moment to calm myself before getting dressed and leaving the bedroom. I didn't want to appear any different until the moment of truth. I didn't want to change too much of the past.

I walked around the bed to the massive closet and found clothes for the day. I couldn't remember exactly what I'd worn that day, but I had a limited selection and chose what I felt would be best. I ended up with a school t-shirt and jeans.

Before I could leave my bedroom and enter the kitchen, my mother had already finished her breakfast and was in the backyard. It was a little early in the season, but I knew she was thinking about her summer garden. She was looking over the area she'd used the previous year for it and was trying to decide if it would be big enough for what she had in mind. Each year she thought it would be big enough then, once everything was planted, she would realize that it wasn't, but it was too late to make changes. If I remembered, I'd give her a suggestion that afternoon to make her think it wasn't big enough and should increase its size.

I ate a quick breakfast of the eggs and bacon mom had already cooked and left on the table for me. It had been a long time since I'd had a decent, home-cooked breakfast, and I relished it, but I didn't waste any time. I ate and gathered my things for school, books all tucked neatly in a backpack and a tattered wallet in my back pocket. I walked to the back door and waved to my mom. She happened to be looking in that direction and returned the wave. It was a routine and nothing needed to be said. The wave was our goodbye. Then I left the house and started on my way to school.

I had typically ridden the school bus and occasionally took my mom's car, but that morning I had walked to school and I would do so that time as well. I didn't recall the significance of that walk, but I still didn't want to change too many things.

A short while later, as I crossed the railroad tracks that ran through the center of town, dividing it into two somewhat unequal sections, I remembered the significance of the walk. That was also the day I encountered the guy that would eventually become my best friend.

Brian Fulton was a big guy, a really big guy, and had been ridiculed because of his weight for years. He was about my height, but outweighed me by at least a hundred pounds, maybe more. I'd never spoken to him before that day. He was a year younger than me and we'd never been in a class together and we ran with different crowds.

That morning, as I took my time walking to school and taking in the sights of the hometown I hadn't visited in over twenty-five years, I noticed Brian trudging slowly up the hill of a narrow side street that led to one of the poorer sections of town. Of course, the area I lived in was maybe a step up from that, but the houses in Brian's section were older and in worse shape. That entire side of town was in bad shape and it only got worse.

I took my time crossing the railroad, looking to my left toward the main rail yard and depot at the multitude of rail cars lined up along the tracks and the haze of smoke and heat rising from the few engines that would soon be pulling those cars northward.

Brian and I reached the same corner at the same time. He was carrying a large sketchpad under his right arm. He practically waddled as he walked and I guess he realized that. He leaned slightly forward to make the waddling motion slightly less pronounced.

As I stepped onto the sidewalk beside him, he looked at me and smiled, his fleshy cheeks rising and his thin lips stretching into nonexistence.

"Good morning," he said cheerfully.

"Morning," I responded and we kept walking.

I matched his pace and tried for a moment to remember what was said before I did something that would damage the beginnings of our friendship. It was the sketchpad under his right arm. That was what I'd commented on and asked about that had triggered our initial conversation.

I pointed at it and said, "I'm guessing you're an artist."

He looked at me and shrugged, "I guess. This is just some stuff for art class."

Brian continued to talk about his artwork and his dream of becoming a comic book artist. I knew a little about that and managed to keep the conversation going for a few blocks. I knew what would happen to him in the future, that he would actually start as a comic book artist and work his way into conceptual art for film companies. He was happy and successful in the future, but I didn't tell him anything about that.

The discussion of art segued into film and science fiction, two topics in which I was more than conversant. That conversation continued until we reached the campus and separated to join our respective groups. I knew then that I had completed that first task of the day and started the friendship with Brian.

While Brian walked toward the rear of the school, I headed for the side entrance near the front of the school. I already saw the guy that was had been my best friend at the time, Darren Ridley.

He was a little taller than I was, and just a little larger. His hair, a perfect styled dark blond, hung to his shoulders and flowed around his soft-featured face. His sea green eyes were rather small and his gaze could be penetrating when he wanted. At that moment, though, his eyes practically sparkled with humor. He was standing with a few other people and apparently relating some humorous incident that he'd discovered on TV.

He gave me a brief nod of the head when he noticed my approach. I returned it slowly, making sure he knew I acknowledged his presence. Darren was a good guy most of the time and we shared some similar interests, but he always seemed to think he was better, smarter, than everyone else around. My grades were just as high as his, and I took harder classes. His primary goal in life was to become a writer. So far, all he'd done was to write a few articles for the school newspaper.

I didn't actually know what happened to him. We went our separate ways after graduation, attending colleges on opposite sides of the country, and we'd lost touch. There had already been two class reunions, one each to commemorate ten and twenty years of our graduation. I hadn't attended either of them. The thirty-year reunion was coming up within the year and I doubted I would attend that one, unless sufficient changes were made. Then I would go to see just how much I would end up changing.

I looked around as I walked toward the side door and around the group of fellow students clustered around it, splintered into groups of five and six, each with their own conversation going. It was in one of those groups that I saw the one person I really wanted to see.

Janet McCann stood with her profile facing me, and it was just as amazing a profile as I remembered. She was absolutely beautiful and I'd wondered if she looked as good nearly thirty years later. I hadn't seen her since the graduation ceremony, but she was the one I'd set as my mental benchmark for beauty. She was tall and lean. She had a dancer's body with long, curly chestnut brown hair, chocolate brown eyes, and a flawless, lightly tanned complexion. She was smiling and that smile actually warmed my heart. I stared at her as I walked toward Darren, but she didn't appear to notice my presence at all. It was what I'd expected, but I knew that would change later in the day.

I finally reached Darren, just moments before the bell rang to start the day. I heard the end of his retelling of something he'd seen on TV the night before, but it didn't make much sense. I'd missed the first part of it and I couldn't remember if I'd ever heard the entire story. He finished as the bell rang and the mass of students began filing toward the doorway, climbing the four steps to the landing then through the metal doors and into the hallway. As we walked, Darren stayed at my side and told me that he needed my help during fifth period to do something for the newspaper. I remembered doing something and I agreed to do it, but I couldn't remember exactly what we'd done. Still, I agreed to it, knowing that my presence was important to my plan.

Inside the building, I had a hard time remembering my schedule, but I found my locker thanks to a girl named Christy Lynch. She was Janet's best friend and sat two rows over from me in first period. My locker was also beside hers. I saw her at the locker and knew where mine was. I walked over to it and opened it without a glance at Christy. She was a little shorter than Janet, with long blond hair and sky blue eyes. She was attractive in her own way, but she was no Janet. She had yet to speak to me and I didn't try to initiate a conversation that morning. I remembered her being rather cold to me throughout high school.

So, I found what I needed for first period and the small stack of papers on the shelf at the top of the locker included a copy of my class schedule. I took that with me, just to make sure.

Then I began the day. I followed the routine and did what I could remember doing. I improvised what I couldn't remember, still hoping that my changes weren't too drastic. I went to English, Calculus, Physics, and Government before lunch. Fifth period was study hall and that left me free to go with Darren on his little excursion.

As it turned out, the task was to pitch an idea to the assistant principal about a fund-raiser for the newspaper. I really didn't have to do or say anything. I was just there for moral support.

Allen Pritchard, assistant principal, was a tall, large man with dark hair fading to gray and receding slightly. He was a former football player and could be rather intimidating at times, but he was generally quite pleasant. He also never let us get away with anything.

He was receptive to Darren's idea and offered some constructive criticism and a few good ideas. Darren, notebook in hand, wrote them all down and agreed to return with a revised form of the plan the following day. I knew that he would and the plan would be accepted. The newspaper would make enough money to continue publication for the remainder of the school year.

The incident I'd been anxiously waiting for occurred on the way back to study hall after the meeting with Mr. Pritchard. I'd wondered briefly if I'd done something in the meeting and had changed the length of it that would affect the timing of the incident afterward. My nervousness about that grew as Darren and I walked along the wide hallway. Darren was excited about the prospect of the fundraiser and expounded on his plan as we walked. I half-listened, but my focus was on what I knew would happen along the way.

I made sure to stay on the right side of the hall. I remembered that much and the entire situation was becoming clearer with each step I took. I looked ahead of me and saw the door where it would occur. I knew what I had to do to make things different and I was ready for it. I took a deep breath as we neared the door and she stepped into the hallway, as if she'd known I would be there. She stepped directly into my path, just as I remembered, and faced me. I pulled up short, stopping just inches from her. The expression on her face was one of desperation and I knew what she was about to say. It had echoed in my mind for over thirty years and I claimed it to be the greatest mistake of my life.

Darren took a couple more steps along the hall before he noticed that I'd stopped. He turned and looked back at me. I waved him on. He nodded and continued walking. I looked at Janet again.

"Paul," she began. "I know we don't know each other, but I really like you."

The first time through that incident, I'd been in a really bad mood, depressed over something inconsequential that I couldn't quite remember. I'd also felt rather unattractive to the females of the school and my first thought was the she was setting me up. I'd pushed her away, denied her advances, and she'd never spoken to me again. I decided to do something different.

"Okay," I said and nodded slowly. "What do you have in mind?"

She relaxed visibly, the tension draining from her shoulders, and she heaved a sigh then said, "Well, maybe we could go out sometime."

"Yeah," I replied. "That sounds good. I really need to get back to class, so how about I call you tonight?"

She smiled and reached into a pocket of her tight jeans. She pulled out a small slip of paper and handed it to me. I took it, our fingers lightly grazing each other, but I didn't look at the paper.

"That's my number," she said. "But call after six-thirty. I'll be done with dinner and homework by then."

She almost giggled. She gave me a quick hug and hurried back into the classroom beside us. I watched her for a second, until she disappeared along a row of desks, then I returned to study hall.

The day ended and I left home, walking back as usual. I looked around for Janet, hoping to just catch a glimpse of her smile before the day ended, but I assumed she had gone to her car in the parking lot at the back of the school. I didn't think I would ever see her again.

As I started toward home, I saw Brian once again, walking in the same direction. I felt rather energized after talking with Janet and basically agreeing to go out with her. Still, I would have to go home and find something to do for the remainder of the night. I knew I would have to leave my younger self a note explaining that he had agreed to a date with Janet. Once I talked to her that night and set up the details, I would leave those for him and he would just have to follow through. I would do my best to make him understand how important that was to the future. I caught up with Brian and started walking alongside him. He looked at me and smiled.

"So, how was your day?" he asked.

I nodded and said, "Pretty good. I accomplished what I planned."

"That's good," he said. "And I even got my art teacher's approval on the drawings I turned in."

"Excellent," I said, knowing that he had done a number of comic book illustrations for a class project. He was proud of that, and pleased.

"So," I said and looked him. "Can I ask you a question?"

"Sure," he said and looked at me.

"What do you think of time travel?"

He thought about it for a second then shrugged and said, "I guess it's conceivable, but there's so much to consider."

"I know," I said with a nod. "Now, I'm going to tell you something that you're not going to really believe. Tomorrow, I won't remember what happened today. But I want you to remind me. Can you do that?"

He nodded slowly and said, "I guess so. But do you mind telling me why you won't remember?"

I thought about it. I didn't remember him telling me anything about time travel, but it's possible that I asked him to keep quiet about that. I knew Brian and knew he would keep his word.

"You promise not to say anything? Not even to me?"

"Yeah," he nodded.

I took a deep breath and said, "It's kind of hard to explain. See, I am from the future, almost thirty years in the future."

He looked at me skeptically and I continued, "Just trust me for now."

He nodded and said, "Okay."

"The only way to really travel in time is to exchange consciousness with another version of yourself. I basically switched minds with my teenage self, but it only lasts one day, from the time I wake up until I go to sleep. So, tomorrow, the guy you talk to won't actually be me, it'll be the seventeen-year-old that should be here. The reason I'm asking you this is because in my original timeline, this is the day we met. Thirty years from now, we're still friends. I don't want that to change."

"Okay," he said. "So why did you come back?"

"Something else happened to me today," I said. "The first time, I did the wrong thing and it affected me for the next thirty years. I came back here to fix that."

"Did you?" he asked.

"Yeah," I nodded. "I think so. Also, if I talk to you tomorrow and say anything about Janet McCann, tell me that I have to go through with it. Can you do that?"

"Sure," he nodded.

I was satisfied that Brian would do what I'd asked him. I trusted him more than any person on the planet.

We parted ways at that point. He turned to head home and I continued on my way alone. I followed through with everything I was supposed to do that afternoon, beginning with the homework I'd been assigned. It was easier than it had been the first time around. Having a number of college degrees made it easy. My mother didn't have any chores for me that day and I did think to remind her about the size of her garden, hinting rather than telling. After dinner, I sat down and began writing the note to my younger self, not finishing it until after my phone conversation with Janet. I wanted to leave him detailed instructions about that more than anything else.

I called her just after six-thirty, as she'd requested. I sort of expected one of her parents to answer the call, but Janet was the one that picked up the phone. We talked for a while about nothing really important, just getting to know each other a little better. Finally, we got around to the proposed date and we made the arrangements for that weekend. We would have lunch on Friday, since I said I had plans for the following day. We would go to the pep rally together Friday afternoon then the game that night. Afterward, we would get something to eat and decide if we wanted to go out again. That was good enough for me.

We finally got off the phone after over an hour. It made sense to me and that point all I could do was hope that my younger self would follow through with it.

I returned to my bedroom and finished writing the message. I left my younger self all the details about the date and what he should do the following day to cover his lack of knowledge. I also told him that Brian Fulton would be his friend and was completely trustworthy. I tried to explain as much as I could about the transference, but I didn't want to go into much detail. Of course, I would figure that out eventually, but I didn't want to start on it too soon. I gave him just enough information to begin his curiosity.

With that written, I took a shower and prepared for bed. I found an old book, one I hadn't read since high school, and started reading it though I knew I wouldn't finish it that night. I made a mental note to look for that book in the future. It had been one of my favorites.
Finally, just after ten, I decided it was time and I began trying to fall asleep. Thankfully, the day had been somewhat emotionally trying and it didn't take long.

When I opened my eyes again, I was looking at a tiled ceiling with twin recessed lighting fixtures that cast a nearly pure white light around the room. I linked a couple of times to adjust to the brightness and a face appeared over me.

I had expected Angela to be there, and she was, but something was different. Her hair was longer and lighter, streaked with blondish highlights. Her skin was a darker tan than I'd ever seen it and she wore pastel colored clothing.

She leaned over the bed and asked, "Did it work? Did you go back and fix it?"

"Yeah," I said and slowly sat up. "Everything should be better now."

I looked around the room and was impressed. The equipment was much nicer than what had been there before. I began detaching the leads from my head and chest that ran to the computer rig beside the bed.

Seated on a chair across from the foot of the bed was an older, but still exquisitely beautiful Janet McCann. She smiled as she looked at me, rising slowly from the chair, and she said, "Glad you're back, honey."

As she stood, I noticed the ring on her left hand. She was married. Then I glanced down at my own hand and saw a ring there as well.

Then it all came to me. I realize now that it was the equivalent of a memory upgrade for a computer. I'd gone to sleep as one person and had awakened as a different person with a different past. Those memories didn't quite take place of my original memories, just sort of coincided with them. It felt like I'd lived two distinctly different lives.

This new one should have been the one that I'd wanted.

I had awakened as a teenager and found a note from myself, detailing all of the things that had happened during that previous day, the one I had no recollection of. I had followed through with the plans I'd made with Janet and that had begun our relationship. It had also inspired me to begin my research into time travel.

Brian and I became friends and remained friends for quite a while, but it hadn't lasted past college. Brian became an artist and became a well-known and well-respected comic book artist and writer. We had sort of drifted apart once Janet and I began dating. Darren and I drifted apart as well. Now, I had a group of friends that were more colleagues than friends.

But I had accomplished the primary goal I'd set for myself and that had been to accept the initial offer from Janet. We had dated through the remainder of high school, gone to college together, and married once we both finished Bachelor's programs. We had two children, a boy and a girl, both in college.

Over the next few days, I learned that more of the world had changed than just my relationship with Janet. I'd lost my best friend and the world was in a depression greater than the one that followed World War One. I won't tell you how horrible this world is. You already know. I just want you to know that it was better before I changed it. I'd successfully traveled through time and changed the past. I know now that it wasn't a good thing and I wondered if I could change it back.

I began working on the theories again, looking for some way to go back and undo what I'd done.

The first idea that came to mind was for a repeat of the previous process. I would travel back to that same date and supplant my other older mind and again reject Janet's offer, but I couldn't quite get a grasp on the mechanics of it, where the consciousness involved would go. It seemed that my younger self would end up in the original older body while that mind would be in the new older body and this mind would be in the younger body. But I couldn't figure out where they would all go once I went back to sleep. That brought me to the idea of parallel universes.

The concept was basically stated in this way: every decision a person makes boils down to a yes or no decision. It's conceivable that for each yes decision there is a no decision that also happens, creating an alternate timeline.

I had created such an alternate timeline, and a much more drastic one than I could've imagined. I had to do something to get out of it. I had what I had dreamed of for thirty years – Janet McCann, but I don't think her presence in my life was worth my soul.

Late one night, I decided to go back to the original date and supplant my parallel self. I did it without Angela's help. I did it on my own.

I've written this just to have a record of those events in case this doesn't work. I want someone to know what happened to me. Maybe someone will find this and read it, maybe not. I just don't know. I just know that I have to try and fix what I did wrong.

All I can do is hope and pray.

RETALIATION

Retaliation is a story of revenge. It's also a story of consequences, reactions, and deception. And it's also something of a statement on bullying, I guess. Maybe the bully in the story and the reactions to the bullying are extreme, but it's all there to make a point. The point is to, in a way, refute the statement that violence never solves anything. Actually, violence solves a great number of things, just not in a positive way.

The five of us beat Randy Evans to a pulp. But that was after we'd knocked out his main flunky, Sid Henderson, and forced his other two friends to run away. Randy was the school bully and had done something to each of us and we'd had all we were going to take from him. We were all seniors and should have been better capable of fending for ourselves, but there was something about Randy that just intimidated us all. Of course, we all felt that we'd been ignored by the system and our concerns were never noted. We had all been pretty much loners until we'd been brought together by the commonality of Randy's torture.

I wanted to be a writer. I fell into all the clichés about writers, but I was definitely not a social creature. I stayed to myself most of the time and watched people. I carried a notebook with me constantly, writing down little details about people and their idiosyncrasies. I made particular note of things people said, wanting to eventually create realistic dialogue.

I apparently watched Randy Evans a little too closely. He noticed me.

I knew quite a bit about him before I ever really started watching him. His reputation had been around for a long time, since we'd all been in grade school and he'd first started beating up the younger kids. I spent at least three years trying to avoid him. He never beat me up in grade school, but more than a few of my friends at the time had been subject to his violent attention. I didn't exactly hide from him. I just went unnoticed, until junior high.

Barely two weeks into the school year, Randy suddenly realized that he had never laid a hand on me. The first time was a simple beating. I left with a bloody nose and aching ribs. After that, it became a bit of extortion laced with the threat of more violence. I acquiesced immediately and I didn't eat lunch for three years. But I wasn't beaten again until high school.

I'd fallen off his radar until the beginning of my senior year, when I'd started watching him with the intent of finding out how a bully operated for a story I had in mind. It actually had nothing to do with Randy, but a bully figured prominently in the plot. Randy noticed and decided I needed a reminder of his physical superiority. After that, I received a reminder about once a month.

The others weren't quite as fortunate.

Ryan Collins was the fat kid. There was no other way to put it. He just liked to eat and always had something on him. Randy had known that for years and began tormenting him followed with extortion for his lunch money and his stash of food. The final straw had been when Ryan had shown up for school one day without any food. Randy had taken that as an act of defiance when it had actually been his mother's idea of a diet. He had been searched before leaving home and every scrap of edible material in his possession had been confiscated. Randy, though, didn't want to understand. He wanted the food and Ryan didn't have it. Randy first beat him senseless then humiliated him by stripping him in the hallway and shoving him naked into the cafeteria at the height of lunch period.

Gary Shaw was the smallest kid in school. He was a senior and still stood barely over five and a half feet tall. He was a good kid and never caused any trouble, but he didn't fit Randy's idea of social norms. That made him a target. But Randy hadn't been the one to inflict the damage on him.

Randy had an entourage that consisted of Sid Henderson, Dave Taylor, and Alison Walker. Dave was the tag-along, the wannabe. Alison was the biggest bitch on campus. She was the perfect feminine complement to Randy. She was damn good looking, but her association with Randy made her less than attractive. Her dark blond hair and sultry, chocolate brown eyes coupled with her full lips and nicely toned body made her physically enticing, but her manner of speech took away anything about her that could possibly be misconstrued as class.

Randy went after Gary and Alison appeared to be his rescuer. She took him away from Randy and convinced him that she was interested. Gary fell for it and she soon had him naked. She'd laughed at him then, with the help of Randy and Dave holding him down, she'd taken a cigarette lighter and burned the hair from his crotch. He hadn't been able to walk comfortable for a week.

Angela Stuart, a girl in the band, was more of a loner than any of us and it was never made clear to me just how she acquired Randy's attention, but his entire group went after her. With Angela, it wasn't just one incident but a series of smaller ones.

The one time Angela had worn a skirt to school, the group of bullies had attacked her before school and removed her panties then spent the rest of the day, since Angela had no way of getting home, lifting her skirt and exposing her to the entire student body. Everyone saw that and Angela had finally gone home in tears at the end of the day.

A few weeks later, Alison sat behind Angela in a class they shared. Alison managed to unhook Angela's bra then followed her to the bathroom when she left the class to fix the situation. Sid had followed them both and, in the bathroom, they had stolen her bra and Sid had taken a few minutes to grope her. Angela had worn a white shirt that day and the group of bullies took every opportunity to douse her with water. Angela spent most of the day walking around with her arms folded across her chest.

The fifth member of our little group, Raven Allen, had received the worst experience of us all and it had been the incident that began our plan of vengeance.

Raven walked home from school every day. She was a small girl, standing just over five feet tall, with long, auburn hair and emerald green eyes. She was a dancer and was somewhat muscular. She looked like she could take care of herself. But Randy and his friends proved that to be a wrongful assumption.

One day, Raven was walking home, her mind on the dance rehearsal she had later that night, and hadn't noticed that she was being followed. They grabbed her, pulled her into a wooded area, and took turns raping her. While the three guys took turns, Alison took pictures. When they finished raping her, they took turns beating her. Then they left her there.

It had taken her over two hours to crawl back to the street and she passed out at the edge of that wooded area. She remained there for nearly another hour before anyone noticed.

She spent two weeks in the hospital.

I barely knew Raven at the time, but I'd decided to visit her in the hospital after several days. Initially, I had wanted to see what a person in the hospital after such an incident actually looked like as research for my potential career as a writer, but after just a few minutes I decided that Raven needed more of a friend than an interviewer.

She'd lost two teeth, had a broken nose, a concussion, two broken ribs, a dislocated hip, and a sprained ankle in addition to the numerous cuts, scratches, and bruises.

After talking to her for a few minutes, I learned that I was the first person to visit her since her parents had been there the day of the incident. They hadn't even returned. She felt forgotten and had almost cried when I walked in the door and sat beside her. I stayed for nearly three hours that first day and went back after school every day after that, spending an hour or two each day, then more and more time on the weekends. We became friends, real friends, during that time, the first real friends either of us had ever had.

Since I had a car and her parents weren't available to drive her home, I picked her up on the Wednesday afternoon when she was discharged from the hospital. A nurse rolled her to the car in a wheelchair, but left me to help her into the car. She was still in pretty bad shape, but much better than when I'd first seen her lying in that bed. I held her the best I could as she transitioned from the wheelchair to the car and she emitted a couple of painful groans, but she was soon in the car and we were on the way to her home.

I drove rather slowly, trying to keep the jarring of the car to a minimum. The shocks on the old Toyota weren't in the best shape and I didn't want to cause her any more injury just for a ride home. I was surprised that her parents hadn't been there to bring her home and she informed me that she was apparently of little importance to them. She said she often felt like a ghost in her own home, just wandering the halls being completely ignored.

A tear rolled slowly down her cheek as she looked at me and said angrily, "I want to make those bastards pay."

I knew how she felt, but I didn't know what she had in mind until she told me.

She turned slightly toward me in the seat, slowly and with a grimace of pain on her face, and said, "I have an idea, but we're going to need some help."

She carefully outlined the plan and I thought it would work.

It took a few more weeks for her health to reach the point where she felt physically able to do anything. She still walked with a slight limp that she had been informed by the doctors that would most likely never go away. Her dancing days were over. But by the time she was ready to execute her plan, I had recruited the people she thought we needed.

The five of us met at Raven's house one afternoon shortly after school, on a day that Randy and his entourage had been rather lenient, to explain Raven's plan.

Ryan and Gary sat on the sofa in the living room with Angela in a chair to their left. I sat in a chair to their right with Raven seated on the arm of the chair.

She looked around at the group then said, "Okay. We're all here because of Randy Evans.

You know what he did to me."

They all nodded, seeming a little embarrassed to know more than they thought they should. I hadn't spread any of the details, but word got around, especially after Randy began bragging about what they'd done.

The only detail Randy had omitted was that Raven had been impregnated. She'd been tested after a few days and the results had been positive. Though she had previously been completely opposed to the concept of abortion, she decided that she was not going to raise Randy's bastard child. She'd been through the procedure a month after leaving the hospital and that had hindered her recovery to the point that our meeting took place with just a few weeks remaining in the school year.

She outlined the plan and the others agreed to participate. There was no reluctance on anyone's part and we put everything on the table. Raven had worked out all the details and apparently she'd learned more about Randy and his entourage than I had. She seemed to know exactly how they would think.

Three days later, we put the plan into action.

Part of Raven's plan was for her to avoid any of that group until that day. She finally walked up to Randy at lunch as he and his buddies were seated on one of the picnic tables outside the main school building. No one else dared go near them. But Raven walked slowly toward the table and the three guys leered at her. Randy smirked, but the smirk turned to an almost angry glare as she stopped in front of them.

"What do you want?" Randy asked.

"I was thinking about what happened," she said and looked at the ground. "I'm kind of embarrassed about this, but I want to see what it's like without the beating."

Randy chuckled and glanced at his friends, "I knew she couldn't get enough of us."

Raven nodded slowly and said, "I was thinking, if you guys didn't have anything else to do, we could meet after school."

"Yeah," Randy laughed. "Meet us at the loading ramp and we'll take care of you."

She nodded in agreement then walked away.

The rest of us skipped our last class of the day and got our things together at the loading ramp. Raven had guessed that was the place Randy would want to meet. It was isolated and typically deserted after school started for the day, unless there was a delivery. She'd really done her homework on that and had a few things already there.

Raven was waiting with her back to the actual loading ramp as Randy and his group arrived. She didn't move as they approached. Randy walked toward her with his right arm around Alison's shoulders. Sid and Dave were just a few feet behind them. We were waiting around the corner of the building.

Randy stopped a few feet from Raven and said, "Okay. We're here. Let's get started. We've got other things to deal with."

She nodded and took a step forward, reaching slowly for the hem of her t-shirt. She started slowly pulling it up. Randy pulled his arm from around Alison's shoulders and rubbed his hands together in anticipation, a lascivious smile on his face. He took a step toward her and she nodded once, the signal for our retaliation to begin.

We all wore gloves, except for Raven, to minimize the evidence if anything legal should come of our plan. We also didn't go into the conflict unarmed. I'd taken a brick from my backyard, from a stalled construction project my father had started and given up on several months earlier. Ryan had a thick rod, a dowel, that he'd wrapped with duct tape and created a handle with electrical tape. Gary had a wooden baseball bat and Angela a couple of large stones she'd taken from the walk in front of her house. Raven told me that she had a surprise and didn't reveal it until after we began the attack.

Gary struck the first blow. He was small, but he was fast. I saw the anger in the narrowing of his eyes and the set of his jaw as he charged Alison. He wanted to make her pay more than Randy. His first blow caught her at the knee. Her leg buckled and she collapsed as Gary stepped past her, turning around as Ryan attacked Dave and I went for Sid.

Ryan struck Dave across the back of the neck, a hard blow that I'm sure would've snapped the dowel had it not been secured with the tape. Dave toppled forward, falling face first to the asphalt drive and his nose took the blunt of the fall. He howled in pain and tried to reach for his injured nose, but Ryan continued his assault, pounding Dave across the back.

I ran up behind Sid and, holding the brick in both hands, broke it across the back of his head. He crumpled to the ground, unconscious.

I looked up as Angela threw her two large stones at Randy. As he dodged the first, looking at Angela, Raven leaned over and quickly picked up a crowbar from beneath a pile of trash.

Angela threw her second stone and it caught Randy full in the face, across the mouth. Both of his lips split and blood shot out, pouring down his chin. He staggered back and I took a step toward them, wanting to help out, but I wasn't needed. Randy took a step toward Angela. Raven stepped up and swung the crowbar with everything she had. The blow landed across the small of his back and I heard something crack. Randy let out a heavy groan then dropped to his knees.

Gary continued his beating of Alison. She'd rolled over and one of his blows caught her in the face, splitting her lip and knocking out a tooth. She covered her face with her hands and Gary still kept striking, grunting with the force of each blow. Alison screamed as the bones of her forearms and hands began snapping. When she rolled on her side, away from him, he stopped swinging.

Ryan stopped beating Dave after a couple of shots. Blood pooled around Dave and Ryan stared at it for a moment. He finally grabbed Dave by the shoulder and lifted him off the ground. Ryan was much stronger than I'd expected, but Dave was also a rather small guy. He climbed to his feet and looked around. His nose was definitely broken, practically flattened, and blood covered his face.

Ryan then spun him around and shoved him toward the opening at the end of the loading bay as he said, "Get the hell out of here."

Raven stepped back from Randy, hefting the crowbar like a baseball bat, and waited as Angela crouched in front of the kneeling Randy. Angela looked him in the eye and said, "I hope this hurts as much as I think it will."

Angela reached between his legs and clamped down. She snarled as her grip tightened and Randy's eyes grew wide. He shook as he fought to keep from screaming, but Angela's grip was more than he could handle. After just a couple of seconds, he let out a howl of pain. Angela held on a few seconds longer then released him. She looked at Raven and nodded.

Gary dropped his bat and rolled Alison onto her back. He smiled at her as he said, "I want you to know just how it feels to be humiliated."

With that, he began taking her clothes off. Part of me wanted to stop him, thinking it had all gone too far, but I remembered everything these people had done to us. I wanted revenge and I wanted it to hurt them as badly as they'd hurt us. It wouldn't be an ongoing thing with us like it had been with them and they needed the full dose at one shot. I did nothing to stop what happened next and I should have. It might have prevented the final results of that ambush, but I stood and watched.

Gary completely stripped Alison, ripping her clothes and tossing them away. She groaned and tried to struggle, but she had a hard time moving. He snarled at her and stood at her feet, staring at her nude body. He stood there only a few seconds then lowered himself and began removing his pants.

As Gary proceeded to have sex with Alison, I looked at Raven and Randy.

She began walking slowly around him as he gripped his crotch with both hands. She looked at him and said slowly, "You raped me, beat me, and left me for dead. And you thought I should just take it because you're Randy Evans and there's nothing anyone can do about it. We'll, I'm doing something about it. I'm going to make you pay for everything you did to me."

He looked up at her and tried to smile, but the remaining pain in his crotch was apparently too much. He let out one brief snort before Raven went into action.

Her first blow was to his midsection. I heard the ribs break and he groaned, but remained on his knees. Raven moved behind him and brought the crowbar down on his ankles. Again, I heard something break and he let out a cry of pain. He started to fall over, but Angela was there to keep him upright as Raven continued.

She stopped in front of him and paused for a few seconds, just staring at him. She then shook her head and said, "You'll definitely never be the same."

She took another swing, this one aimed at his jaw, and he fell to the side, physically unable to let out a scream through his broken jaw and shattered teeth. Angela then lifted him back to a kneeling position. Raven walked around behind him and said, "You wanted me on my back so I'm going to make sure you stay on yours."

With that, she swung again, aiming again at his lower back. The metal struck his flesh with a heavy thud and he pitched forward, his eyes closing. He didn't move. I at first thought he was dead, but I looked closely and saw that he was still breathing.

Ryan then walked up to me and placed a hand on my shoulder. I looked at him and he said softly, "We should get out of here."

I nodded and walked toward Raven. She looked up at me and smiled proudly.

We left the school with Randy lying on the ground, severely injured and unmoving, Sid not far away and starting to recover, and Alison naked and crying several feet away. I felt bad for their condition, but not for them. They got what they deserved.

None of them said anything. They claimed to have not seen their attackers. And they were out of school for quite a while.

Dave had suffered the least of them. He had left with a shattered nose, a sprained neck, and a few scrapes. Sid had a major concussion and a few scrapes. Alison had a dislocated knee, two broken arms, three broken bones in her hands, a dislocated jaw, numerous bruises, and had lost two teeth.

Randy had received the worst of it all. His jaw had been shattered and he'd lost six teeth. Three ribs had been broken and his spleen and one kidney had ruptured. One of his testicles had been crushed and his left ankles had been broken. But the worst injury of all had come as a result of Raven's final blow. She had broken his back and he was paralyzed from the waist down.

We appeared to have gotten away with it, but it wasn't enough for Raven. She was still angry and thought the damage she'd inflicted on Randy hadn't been enough. She thought he deserved more.

Raven and I sort of became a couple after that, as did Ryan and Angela. I still wasn't sure we were dating, but we spent a lot of time together. The five of us had definitely become friends and that was something. We just didn't know where to go from there.

The school year ended and we all graduated with plans on attending the local community college. Sid and Dave recovered from their injuries first. Sid joined the army and left town less than a month after graduation. Dave just disappeared a few days after Sid left.

Alison slowly recovered and tried to make amends. It was painful for all of us, but she began to become a nicer person. Her looks were gone, thanks to Gary, and she couldn't rely on them to get by any longer. She didn't quite become our friend, but we no longer felt any real animosity toward her. She left for college in another state at the end of the summer and I never saw her again.

Randy returned to the public eye a couple of months after we'd started college. I ran into him on the street near the high school on a Saturday afternoon in early October. He was in a wheelchair.

He stopped in my path and glared up at me as I stopped a few feet away and finally looked at him.

We stared at each other uncomfortably for a few minutes and he finally broke the silence.

"You guys really took care of us," he said. "That was harsh."

"Yeah, well…" I stammered.

"It's okay," he said and visibly relaxed. "We deserved it. Hell, we deserved it ten times over. Look, I'm sorry for everything. I don't expect you to forgive me. I just want you to know how I feel."

He leaned slightly forward, the best he could, and continued, "The other guys, Sid, Dave, and Alison, were all just following my lead, you know? It really wasn't their fault, but they did what they did. Anyway, I just wanted you to know. Take care of yourself."

With that, he moved the chair around me and disappeared down the sidewalk.

I told Raven about it and she seemed a little disturbed that he was back in town. She'd sort of expected him to be placed in some sort of special facility for a long time. I didn't understand why she still held so much anger toward him. And I definitely didn't expect her reaction to the news of his return.

Two days later, I found out.

Raven found Randy and got him alone in a park a few blocks from the school. I found out when I returned home and there was a message from her on my home voice mail. She hadn't called my cell phone at all. She told me that she was meeting Randy to make amends and settle their differences once and for all. The tone of her voice suggested that she was sincere in planning to accept his apology and forgive him, but I knew Raven better than that. She was going to do something drastic.

I ran out of the house and drove as fast as I could to the park. It was a fairly large park and it took me a few minutes to locate Randy and Raven. They were in a secluded, deserted area of the park. I walked quickly toward them and watched as they faced each other, talking animatedly.

I was within shouting distance as I saw Raven reach into her purse and pull out a small pistol. She stepped forward, placed the pistol against his forehead, and pulled the trigger.

Randy's head snapped back and portions of his head splattered the ground behind it. I screamed and Raven turned toward me.

I was close, almost close enough to do something, but far enough away that she had time to follow through with her final act.

She said loudly, "I'm sorry."

I took a deep breath, ready to scream, but she quickly raised the pistol to her temple and pulled the trigger. Her lifeless body fell to the ground and Randy's feet.

I realized later, after much thought and a discussion with the others in the group, that Raven had been planning that since the day she'd awakened in the hospital after having been raped. She wanted them all to pay, but Randy more than the others. Her entire life after that moment had been lived with a single purpose and she'd achieved that. She'd killed Randy Evans. At that moment, her life had been over. She'd reached the point she'd seen as the culmination of her life's work. She'd taken out the bully and she had planned all along to pay for that prize with her life. The humiliation of the rape, the beatings, the pictures, and the abortion had pushed her over the edge and vengeance had consumed her.

In the end, the relationship I'd been counting on with her had been nothing more than a step in the process of exacting her revenge. I had been a mere stepping stone and had meant nothing to her. That hurt more than anything else.

THE ESCAPE

The Escape is yet another vampire story and sort of serves as an introduction to the Dead Time novels. It's not exactly a lead-in, but the location and situations fit with it rather well.

The story itself was inspired by an incident that actually happened when I was in high school. There were no vampires and I wasn't actually involved in the incident, but I was around it at the beginning and the latter portions were revealed to me later by one of the people involved. Yes, great exaggeration and alteration took place.

It's kind of a long story, almost novella length, but I like it and here it is.

ONE

Houston wasn't quite as big of a city in 1981 as it is today, but it was big enough for the four of us to get lost. We'd been on the road nearly twelve hours when we pulled into the city, almost out of gas and completely out of food. The only thing remaining in the small Isuzu car was a six-pack of warm beer. We'd already been through plenty of that and all the food we could afford. The problem was that we'd run out of money before crossing the Texas border from Louisiana. We'd wanted to make it as far as possible from our hometown of McLain, Mississippi, possibly all the way to the west coast, but Houston was the best we could do without any planning.

It started with a bad idea and thankfully it hadn't been my idea. I'd just been dumb enough to go along with it.

It was homecoming week at McLain high school and three of us were seniors. Johnny Morris and Mitch Barksdale had been friends since elementary school. I'd only been in McLain since sixth grade, but those two had been the first friends I'd made after moving from Georgia. As our senior year started, we were practically inseparable. Linda Hewitt was the fourth, a junior that enjoyed most of the same things we enjoyed. She was pretty much a wild child and I didn't have a problem with that.

Mitch instigated the whole thing. The idea was for us to meet early in the morning and do a little drinking before school started. We'd made it through the week without getting caught, until Friday. Mitch had gone a little overboard with the drinking that morning and before first period had even started we'd been called to the principal's office.

The four of us sat in folding metal chairs facing the massive desk that occupied most of the office. Lawrence Davis kept his office neat and tidy with no excess decorations. The only things on any of the walls were his diplomas. He had one filing cabinet and his desk. The rest of the office remained bare space.

He sat behind that desk and glared at us for several long moments, leaning forward with his forearms resting on the immaculate surface of the desk and his fingers laced together. Mr. Davis was a tall, large black man with neatly trimmed black hair that was beginning to fade to gray at the temples. His dark eyes were narrowed as his gaze ticked back and forth along the row of us. Linda and I sat up fairly straight, more concerned about the consequences of getting caught than either Johnny or Mitch. Johnny sat back against the chair while Mitch practically lounged in his.

Finally, Mr. Davis sat up and placed his hands on the arms of his black leather chair then said, "I must say that I'm disappointed, especially in you three seniors. You should be setting proper examples for the younger students and definitely not encouraging this sort of behavior."

Mitch shook his head slowly, "So, what's going to happen now? How much detention do we get?"

David looked at him and shook his head slowly, "No detention. In fact, I'm not going to issue any punishment for any of you. I'll let your parents make that decision, after consulting the authorities."

That caused Mitch to sit up. He leaned forward and his gaze narrowed slightly, "The authorities?"

"Yes," Mr. Davis said with a nod. "You and Johnny are both eighteen and no longer considered minors, despite the fact that you're still in high school. By providing Linda and Evan with alcohol, you've committed a crime. I have no alternative other than to contact the authorities."

Mitch shook his head and sat up straight, "That's a load of crap! Half the class does it and it's not hard for anyone to get it if they know the right places."

Mr. Davis leaned back, "I'm sorry, Mitch, but that's all I can do. Mrs. Lambert will be making the calls to your parents and the police shortly. I suggest you think about what you've done and be on your best behavior. This may just blow over, but not if you present the town officials with the attitude you're showing me here."

Johnny shook his head and looked away, "Do what you got to do."

Mr. Davis pushed his chair back and stood up. He stared at us a second longer, shaking his head, then walked out of the room, presumably to start the process of making the calls.

As soon as the door, to our left, closed, Mitch looked at Johnny and said, "He's serious, man. We've got to do something."

Johnny looked at him, his own chocolate brown eyes going wide, and asked, "Like what? We can't hide from this."

Mitch was silent for a second, nodding thoughtfully, then smiled and said, "But we can get the hell out of here."

I frowned and looked at Mitch, "What are you talking about?"

Mitch looked at me and grinned, "We got Johnny's car. I've got some money at home. We run the hell out of here and just take off. By the time they find us, they'll be glad enough to have us back that they'll forget all about this crap."

"I don't know," I said weakly and shook my head.

Linda, on the other hand, sat up straight and smiled, "That's perfect. But how do we get out of here, out of this office."

Mitch chuckled, "He didn't lock us in. We just open the door and run."

A few moments later, we'd all sort of gone along with the plan. I was a little reluctant to take part, but I didn't see that I had much choice. I wasn't going to hold my friends back and I wasn't going stay behind and take it all myself.

We moved to the door. Mitch slowly turned the knob and pulled the door open a couple of inches, just enough to see through, and leaned in close. After a couple of seconds, he opened it a little wider and stuck his head out. He looked back and forth then pulled back into the room.

He smiled and said softly, "It's pretty clear. Davis is talking to Mr. Thompson in the corner. Mrs. Lambert is in back on the phone, probably calling our parents. No better time."

Without another word, Mitch pulled the door open all the way and we made a run for it. The outer office was a good bit larger than the principal's inner office, which was near the front corner, beside the main counter that separated the working area from the visiting area, where students and visitors waited to be seen. The end of the counter was a flip up section just wide enough for a single person to walk through. Mitch, the first one out of the inner office, reached the counter and flipped the section upward with enough force that it flopped back and slammed into the main counter, the slapping sound practically echoing through the room. He ran through and we were right behind him. No one was in the visiting area and provided no impedance to our exit. Mitch shoved the outer door open and shot to his right. We followed, leaping down the few steps at the end of the hallway to the door that led to the outside and to our freedom.

From there, with the shouts of Mr. Davis chasing after us, we ran along the sidewalk at the side of the school toward the main parking lot across a narrow street from the city block that the campus occupied. As we reached the corner of the building, its white brick fading and dull, I saw Johnny's small, silver-gray car parked at the edge of the lot barely twenty yards south of the corner. Mitch, still in the lead, cut across the grassy area at the corner of the campus and shot across the street.

A moment later, we were piling into the car. Johnny unlocked the driver's side door and leaned in far enough to unlock the passenger's side door. Mitch and Linda had run to that side and I'd stayed with Johnny. Once Johnny pulled out of the car and shoved the back of the seat forward, I dove inside. On the other side, Mitch had done the same and Linda dove in, landing practically on top of me. Mitch and Johnny climbed in and before Linda and I could untangle our limbs and sit up, Johnny had the car started and in motion. Tires screeched against the asphalt of the lot as he turned right and accelerated. I managed a glance outside just in time to see Mr. Davis stop near the corner of the campus and heave a sigh.

Mitch was laughing and had one hand on the dashboard, his grin almost maniacal.

TWO

Our first stop was at Mitch's house on the south side of town. We pulled up to the curb beside the ramshackle dwelling that looked like it was ready to collapse on itself, from what we could see of it from the street. The front was practically hidden from view by the overgrowth of bushes and plants haphazardly scattered across the small front yard.

As the car stopped, Mitch looked at Johnny and said, "Wait here. Give me five minutes. If anybody shows up, take off and I'll meet you at Grady's Quick Stop."

Johnny nodded and Mitch hurried out of the car. He closed the door and looked back and forth quickly then ran toward the front of the house, leaping up the three steps that led to the front porch. At that point, he was out of sight.

I looked at Johnny and said, "I don't know if this is such a good idea."

Johnny looked over his shoulder at me, "It might not, but it's better than going to jail, don't you think?"

I shrugged and sat back. I wasn't yet eighteen and I wasn't going to jail over the incident. I knew I could walk away and receive only a relatively minor punishment for my actions, but I wasn't going to leave my friends.

Linda then laughed lightly and wrapped both of her arms around my right. She looked up at me, her sea green eyes wide and pleading, her lean face surrounded by a mass of dark blond curls, and said, "Come on, Echo, we'll be fine. Look at it as one more adventure."

Echo. That was a name I hadn't heard in a while. It was a shortening of my name, Evan Cole. It had happened shortly after my arrival in McLain and it had stuck for a while, but had been more or less relegated to the past when we entered high school. Linda's sudden use of it and the almost amorous look in her eyes made me forget about trying to leave and let some of the tension and anxiety over our situation fade away.

Linda was a damn good looking girl, fairly tall, and with a body that was just amazing. As she leaned against me, I felt the soft pressure of her left breast pressing against my arm and that was enough for me to give up whatever thoughts of going back and facing the music I'd had to vanish.

Johnny sat in the front with one hand draped almost casually over the steering wheel and kept glancing in the rearview mirror and looking over his shoulder when he wasn't consulting the gleaming gold watch on his left wrist.

Johnny Morris was the son of local physician and surgeon Dr. James Morris. That meant he had no worries about money. The car had been paid for and was actually in Johnny's name, not his father's. He was the only one in the class that officially owned his own vehicle. I didn't have one at all and neither did Mitch. But Johnny was always there, always available, when we needed a ride. And he was always up for just about anything.

A couple of minutes later, Mitch came running out of the house with a backpack slung over his shoulder and a case of beer in his hands. As he approached the car, Johnny leaned over and opened the door. Mitch used his right foot to push it all the way open then leaned in and handed the beer to me over the seat. He then climbed in and closed the door, laughing.

Once the door was closed, Johnny put the car into gear and pulled away from the curb.

"I got a little over a hundred bucks," Mitch said and dropped his backpack to the floor between his feet. "How much you guys got?"

I shrugged, "About twenty, I guess."

Linda shook her head, "I'm broke."

Johnny smiled, "I can get a check cashed, probably get another couple hundred."

"Let's do it," Mitch said. "We're gonna need gas and food."

"I got it," Johnny said and snapped the fingers of his left hand. "We go to Grady's and fill up. I'll write a check and get the extra money there."

"Excellent," Mitch said and laughed almost giddily.

A few minutes later, we were stopped beside the pumps at Grady's Quick Stop near the edge of town. We'd been there on numerous occasions to buy beer and other necessities. We were regulars and Mr. Grady, the owner and primary operator, knew us well.

I pumped the gas while Johnny went in to pay for the gas and get some extra cash. Linda went to the bathroom and Mitch gathered a few more supplies, mostly snacks and an extra twelve-pack. Ten minutes later, we were on the road.

THREE

We had no idea where we were going at first, but we were headed west. A couple of hours later, taking winding back roads, we found ourselves in Baton Rouge. We stopped for lunch and used some of our precious cash to pay for it. The restaurant wouldn't take an out-of-state check from Johnny. Then we were back on the road and headed toward Texas.

Somewhere along the way, as we talked, the idea of going as far as California entered the conversation.

"Yeah," Mitch said. "That'd be great. We can hit Hollywood and actually do something."

"I don't know," I said. "That's a stretch. I think we'll be lucky to make it through Texas."

We barely made it into Texas.

We filled the tank again, bought more food, and drank most of the beer, even the warm stuff Mitch had taken from his house.

We reached Houston and just drove around for a while with no real destination in mind. It began to get late and we thought about finding a place to sleep. Johnny's first suggestion was to find a motel, but Mitch had another idea.

"Motels are too expensive," he said. "I think we can find a shelter where we can sleep for free."

He went on to explain that he had a cousin that had been in Houston a few years earlier, the cousin that we'd learned just hitchhiked around the country with no permanent home, and he had spent a few nights in one of the shelters. He said it wasn't great, almost like a prison at times, but it was free and there was free food, though not the best in the world.

"All we gotta do is look like we're down on our luck," he said. "We'll find the place, park the car somewhere else, leave all our stuff in it, and walk up to the place."

I had no idea how we were going to even find the place, but Mitch directed Johnny to a seedy section of town, apparently following directions his cousin had given him, and soon found a shelter.

It was the Wayfarer's Rest Shelter and was on the very southern edge of Houston. We didn't see any place nearby that we thought would be a safe place to leave the car with all our belongings and spent over an hour looking. Johnny finally located a spot about three miles from the shelter and that was where we parked. We took everything out of our pockets and left it in the car. The only thing we brought was the key to the car.

I felt almost naked as we walked away from the car without anything other than the clothes on my back. I still had a few bucks and there was maybe a hundred left from the stash accumulated by Johnny and Mitch. It was well hidden in the car, but we planned on being back in the vehicle the following morning. The only comfort I felt in the situation was that as we started walking, Linda fell in step beside me and wrapped her arms around my right arm once again.

We were tired, but we kept going. It was after eleven when we left the car and we reached the shelter shortly after midnight. Linda was still holding onto my arm as we walked up to the front door in a recessed section of the brick building. Mitch tried the door and found it locked. He leaned in close and read the faded sign taped to the glass upper portion of the door. He snickered and reached for the doorbell button beside the door. He pressed it and we waited. A few moments later, the door opened and we were greeted by a guy, a couple of inches shorter than I was, with short, dark blond hair that was thinning on top and shining brown eyes. He wore jeans and a red t-shirt. He smiled, a seemingly genuine smile, and pulled the door open wide.

"Hi," he said warmly. "I'm Steve Hollister. What can I do for you?"

Mitch, the architect of the plan, stuffed his hands into the pockets of his own jeans and said, "We've had a little trouble and need a place to crash for the night."

Steve nodded and stepped back, "Well, that's what we're here for. Come on in."

We entered a narrow hallway that smelled of mold, sweat, and something I couldn't quite identify. It wasn't overpowering, but it was there. I was the last one in, ushering Linda through the door way with my right hand gently on her back just above the hem of her lightweight blue jacket. Steve stood at the door, smiling, and closed the door behind us. I glanced back as I heard the click of a lock being engage and saw him pulling a key from the lock.

"Sorry," he said. "But you guys just made it. We're locking up for the night."

He shifted past us, moving sideways with his back to the wall, the smile still on his face.

He reached the front of the group and faced us then said, "Look, I'm on my way out for the night. Give me a minute and I'll have my assistant take care of you."

We nodded. He turned and started quickly down the hallway. He took a couple of steps then looked over his shoulder and said almost too anxiously, "Just wait right there."

He then disappeared into the shadows of the hallway. It was fairly dark in there, but there was enough light filtering through the filthy glass of the doors to allow us to see each other, if little else.

Mitch looked at us, smiling, and said, "See? I told you this would work."

Johnny shrugged. Linda took my arm again and I felt her shiver slightly. It wasn't really that cold, but was apparently enough for her.

We stood there only a couple of minutes and we heard footsteps down the hallway. I peered into the darkness and saw motion, but it wasn't clear to me what was happening until the source of the motion stepped into the dim light.

She was beautiful and exotic. She was a little taller than Linda and wore all black. Her hair, perfectly straight and shoulder-length, was as black as the night sky and her narrow features were wrapped in a dark complexion. Her eyes, twin points of gleaming black, held little humor in them. She smiled and her perfect teeth shone in the darkness.

She stopped a few feet from Mitch and said, "Hi. I'm Karen Brody. Steve told me your situation and we'll be glad to give you a place for the night, but you have to understand that we have a few rules."

Mitch nodded, "Whatever you say."

She glanced at him and nodded, "Good. This won't take long. Follow me."

She turned curtly and started walking along the hallway. Mitch tossed us a shrug and followed. We followed him.

The hallway was longer than I'd expected and ended at a heavy door. Karen stopped and pulled a set of keys from a pocket of her skin-tight pants. She unlocked the door and pulled it open.

The room beyond the door was brightly lit and we all flinched at the sudden appearance of the light. Karen didn't seem to be bothered by it. Apparently she had been in a well-lit room and her eyes hadn't adjusted to the darkness enough for this light to bother her. She walked through the door and we followed.

The room was large and white. The walls were painted white and the floor was made of square white tiles. There were two more doors in the room, one set into the walls on either side of us. An old, wooden table sat on the floor on each side of the door we'd entered with a few cabinets above each table.

Karen had stopped just inside the door we'd entered and pulled it closed once we were inside. As it closed, we turned to face her.

She looked even better in the light. The tight clothing displayed an amazing body, possibly even better than Linda's. She moved closer, her walk more sinuous than I'd expected, and my eyes were drawn to her.

As she moved, she said, "This may seem a little insensitive, but it's the policy we've been forced to institute. Health and hygiene issues are frequently problematic in places like this, so, we insist on everyone entering to shower before entering the residence area."

Mitch grinned and said, "We've just been on the road. We haven't been on the streets."

Karen cocked her head almost condescendingly to one side and said, "I'm sorry, but I have to follow the rules."

She pointed to the open doorway to our right and said, "That's the shower room. I'll need you to all disrobe and leave your clothing on the table behind you."

I frowned, "You mean we're all showering together?"

She nodded, "Yes. And I'll be supervising, to make sure you are clean. I know it's weird, but it's the policy."

Then she started taking her clothes off. Once her long-sleeved shirt was pulled over her head and her large, pale breasts were revealed, Mitch and Johnny immediately began disrobing. I was a little slower to react and Linda looked up at me. I could see in her eyes that she was uncomfortable with the situation, but we apparently had no choice, especially if we wanted a place to sleep that night.

With a shrug, I started taking my own clothes off. Linda reluctantly did the same. Karen was naked before any of us. She wore only the shirt and pants over slim black shoes, no underwear. Mitch and Johnny stared at her. I finished undressing and waited for Linda, holding her hand for balance as she pulled her panties from her ankles.

As we gathered our clothes and placed them in separate piles on the table, Karen walked to the shower room, turned on the light with a switch beside the entrance, and walked inside. She turned on the water and we walked in.

She stood at the center of the room with her hands on her hips and her feet spread slightly. There were six shower heads spaced around the room, two on each of three walls. The two on the wall across from the entrance were not on, just the four on the side walls. We moved in and started the showering process. Mitch and Johnny moved to the right. Linda and I moved to the left.

I began the process, as did the others. Soap and shampoo were there, resting on a small shelf set into the wall below the shower head, and I started with the soap. A few seconds later, I heard a slight yelp from Linda a few seconds later. I looked over and saw that Karen stood behind her with a thick cloth in her hands, helping Linda with her shower. Linda looked over her shoulder and Karen said softly, "Trust me. This is my job."

I didn't expect her to go any farther, but a few moments later, I felt her hands on me. She held the cloth in one hand, but her bare hand massaged my back for a moment then reached around. Her hand was cool and soft as it moved expertly over my damp flesh. Of course, I reacted, but she didn't seem to notice. She was only there a few moments, but it was enough. When her hands left me and she moved away, I felt that something important had been taken away from me.

She moved then to Johnny and finally to Mitch. When she finished with Mitch, she declared that we were clean enough for the Wayfarer's Rest.

We left the shower room and Karen pulled towels from the cabinet above the table. We spent a few moments drying ourselves then started for our clothes.

"Not so fast," Karen said and moved between us and out belongings, still naked. "We can't allow you to put those back on. We normally have some of our workers bring in clothing, but it's late and they're all gone for the day. So, if you'll follow me, we'll find you something to wear."

I didn't relish the thought of walking through this facility completely naked, but there wasn't much choice. We followed her and we weren't quite surprised when she made no move to dress herself. She just opened the other door in the room and walked through it.

FOUR

The available clothing consisted only of medical scrubs, obviously used and re-used, but clean. We were each provided with a pair of pants, a top, and a pair of slip-on shoes. No underwear or socks were available. We stood in the narrow hallway outside the large closet where the garments were stored and dressed. It didn't take long.

She then led us deeper into the building, to a fairly large room with several narrow bunks that consisted of thin mattresses on metal frames with loose strands of metal wire strung from side to side. A single pillow rested at the head of each bed. There were eight beds in the room and only two were occupied. An old man lay on his back in the far right corner of the room and a girl was curled up on the bed in the far left corner.

Karen, now wearing scrubs as well, stood at the door and said softly, "Take any bed you'd like. We'll wake you up at seven for breakfast."

With that, Karen was gone. She slipped away silently and left us alone.

Linda grabbed my hand and pulled me to the left, toward the bed where the girl lay sleeping. Mitch and Johnny took beds on the other side of the room, close to the door. Linda led me to a bed in the corner and sat down. I started to back away, but Linda held onto my hand and looked up at me.

"I don't want to be alone," she said softly, glancing furtively at Mitch and Johnny as they settled into their bunks. "Just stay here with me."

"Okay," I replied with a nod and settled onto the bed beside her.

She leaned back and shifted into the corner, her back against the wall. She looked much like a scared child as she grabbed the single pillow and wrapped her arms around it then tucked it under her head. I felt a small smile creep across my face. She just looked so adorable like that.

I reached over to the next bed and grabbed the pillow from it then crawled into bed beside her. She reached out with one hand, grabbed my arm, and pulled me closer to her. I shifted closer and let my left arm fall across her back. She rolled against me and closed her eyes.

I felt strange about being in the place and the things we'd already had to go through, but I was exhausted and needed sleep. I closed my eyes and was asleep in moments.

FIVE

I woke up and realized somewhat instinctively that something was wrong. I'd never slept that much, maybe six hours a night, and it had been after one before we'd been taken to our beds. That meant it had to be seven at the earliest. My watch had been included with my clothes, so I didn't know exactly, but I was pretty good at guessing the time. But the only thing I was certain of at that time was that Linda was still snuggled against me.

I'd never before considered Linda to be anything more than a friend, just part of our little group. She was a drinking buddy and a girl I could actually talk to without feeling like a complete fool. We'd spent a lot of time together, mostly with Johnny and Mitch, rarely just the two of us, and I felt comfortable with her. Now, though, I began to feel a little differently about her at that point. I wouldn't have said that I had been ready to marry her or even date her, but I saw her differently that morning, as something more than merely a friend. I guess I was feeling a little protective after the way she'd held onto me all night and seemed to so desperately want me to hold her through the night.

I didn't want to wake her. I'd had my rest, but she'd told me that she liked to sleep late. I would let her sleep until Karen or Steve came to wake us for breakfast. I lay there beside her a few moments longer, relishing the closeness and letting those feelings wash over me before reality set in and changed everything. Then I eased away from her, partially rolling toward the edge of the bed, and looked to see if Johnny and Mitch were awake yet.

They were gone.

It looked as if those beds hadn't been slept in at all, but that was hardly any indicator. The beds were bare mattresses, but there appeared to be no indentations on the pillows. It was definitely possible that either they'd returned the pillows to their original condition, but highly unlikely, or that someone had come along and done that for them.

I slowly extracted myself from Linda's embrace and sat up carefully, still not ready to wake her.

As I sat up, I noticed the girl in the far corner sitting up on her bed. She wore the same pale blue scrubs that Linda and I both wore. Her long, chestnut brown hair was something of a tangled mess and she was trying to straighten it out with her fingers. After a few seconds, she stood up and started toward me. She reached the bed and crouched beside it, looking up at me. She was absolutely beautiful.

"You guys came in last night?" she asked, her voice deep and rich.

"Yeah," I nodded.

"Were those two guys with you?"

I nodded and she shook her head.

"I'm sorry," she said. "I don't think you're going to see them again."

I frowned and leaned a little closer, "What do you mean?"

"I've been here a few days," she said and looked around furtively. "There have been several people come in, but they always disappear before breakfast call and they're never seen again."

I shrugged, "Maybe they just left."

"No," she shook her head again. "You can't just leave. They keep the doors locked, except for the outside door, but you can't get to that. There's some weird crap going on here."

Our conversation woke Linda. She sat up, rubbed her eyes, and wanted to know what was going on. I told her quickly about the disappearance of Johnny and Mitch then started to introduce her to the girl, but I didn't know her name. So, I asked.

"Mallory," she said and moved to the bed beside us. "Mallory Thorne. I came here from Oklahoma looking for work."

I nodded, introduced myself and Linda then said, "We're from Mississippi, sort of running from the law."

Mallory looked shocked, her big, brown eyes growing even wider, and I explained our situation quickly. She still didn't seem to fully understand, but that didn't matter. I began to grow nervous, wondering what had happened to Johnny and Mitch.

Breakfast call came a few minutes later. Steve stuck his head in the door and announced it in a relatively calm voice that we were to follow him to the dining area. Linda, Mallory, and I stood up and started for the door. The old man in the other corner remained in his bed, not moving at all.

At the door, I looked at Mallory and asked, "Shouldn't we wake him up?"

Mallory shook her head, "Nah. He's been here longer than I have and I've never seen him leave that bed."

It was strange, but I didn't question her about it. Besides, we were falling behind and I realized just how hungry I was. We entered the hallway and followed Steve, away from the shower room.

The dining area was a fairly large room near the end of the hall with four large tables at the center and a single counter along one wall. The aroma of bacon, eggs, toast, and coffee filled the room and wafted into the hall. I could feel my mouth watering at the thought and didn't think twice as I walked into the room and Steve stood beside the door, smiling.

"Have at it, guys," he said cheerfully. "Eat all you want."

There was a stack of plates and a tray of silverware at one end of the counter. I picked up a plate and a set of silverware then started filling the plate. Linda and Mallory moved in behind me. I felt a little guilty for grabbing food first, but I did it quickly and they didn't complain.

A few moments later, we were seated at one of the tables and I started eating ravenously, as if I hadn't eaten in days. Linda and Mallory did pretty much the same. Steve was the last to sit with his plate, which wasn't quite as full as ours, and he ate slowly. I was sure he'd seen behavior like ours before, probably on a regular basis, and most likely thought nothing of it. I ate voraciously for a few moments until the pangs of hunger subsided somewhat then looked at Steve and said, "I noticed that my two buddies weren't there this morning. Do you know what happened to them?"

Steve nodded through a mouthful of eggs and chewed through it before he replied, "Of course. They had trouble sleeping and left the room. Karen took them out back to our little garden. They've been working a little bit for us."

I nodded, thinking it kind of strange that those two would easily consent to working in a garden when I knew that neither of them had ever seen a real garden, much less done any work in one.

"Have they had breakfast?" Linda asked then shoveled another strip of bacon into her mouth.

"Yes," Steve said and looked at her. "They ate a little over an hour ago."

Then he looked at me and said, "I guess Karen didn't explain this last night, but we really can't provide food and lodging at no charge."

We all stopped eating and looked at him. He sat back and held his hands up.

"Don't get me wrong," he said, still smiling. "We're not asking for money. All we ask is that you do a little work for us before you leave. Your two friends are doing their share. I'm sure an hour or two isn't too much to ask."

"No," I said with a shrug. "I guess not."

"Fine," Steve said and pushed his chair back. "I'll go get things ready and come back to get you in a few minutes."

He stood and walked away, leaving his plate on the table.

Once he was gone, Mallory looked at me and said, "I think there's something more to it than just working in a garden for a while."

I nodded, "So do I. But we don't have much choice right now."

She shrugged, "We could just get the hell out of here."

"No," I shook my head. "Not without Johnny and Mitch."

She took a deep breath and nodded.

SIX

Steve did return a few minutes later and escorted us to a fairly large courtyard at the back of the building. He gave us each a pair of gloves and told us that all he wanted was for us to pull some weeds. The area was maybe twenty feet on a side, so four hundred square feet. When we were done with that, we had paid our debt and could do as we pleased.

Before Steve left, I looked at him and asked, "What about Johnny and Mitch? I thought they were here."

"No," he shook his head. "They're at another garden. They should be done about the same time you are."

Before I could ask anything else, he excused himself and left, closing the door behind him. I waited a few seconds then tried the door. It was locked. The courtyard was surrounded on all four sides by three-story brick walls and no windows. We were there until Steve decided to let us leave.

We did as we were asked and started pulling weeds. There were quite a few of them and it took the three of us well over an hour to finish the job. When we were done, we sat on the ground beside the door and waited for Steve. Linda sat on my right and Mallory on my left. We were tired and sweaty, but it felt good to have actually done some work. We sat there silently for a few minutes, catching our breath, until Mallory broke the silence.

"I don't think this is it," she said. "I think they're going to come up with some reason to keep us here."

"Yeah," Linda chimed in. "It's really creepy here. We never should've listened to Mitch."

I agreed with her. The whole situation was really Mitch's fault. It had been his idea to do all the drinking before school, his idea to run away from the situation, his idea to drive west, and his idea to seek accommodations at the shelter. The blame was definitely his, but I wasn't going to leave him holding the bag. Any or all of us could have said something, but we went along with it blindly. Now, we had to figure out our next move.

"We have to find our clothes," I said after a couple of minutes.

Linda looked at me and asked, "Why?"

I looked at her, "The car key. It's in Johnny's pocket. We need that key to get out of here. We get that, get Johnny and Mitch, and haul it out of this town."

"Then where do we go?" Linda asked.

"Home," I said and she looked away, staring at the wall in front of her.

Mallory looked at me and said, "That's great for you guys, but I don't have anywhere to go."

I frowned, "What do you mean? I thought you were here from Oklahoma looking for work."

"Yeah," she said and heaved a sigh. "That's sort of the truth."

Then she told me her story.

SEVEN

Mallory Thorne left Tulsa, Oklahoma less than a year after her parents had died in a house fire. She had been at school at the time of the fire, a junior in high school, and had been unaware of the incident until school ended for the day and she'd arrived at her home to find two fire trucks and three police cars parked around the charred ruins of her home.

She had no other relatives to take her in and she'd spent just over a year shifting from foster home to foster home. She'd hated every minute of it, but she'd stuck with it long enough to get a job and save a little money. When she finally thought she had enough to do something with, she'd walked away from Tulsa and started hitching south.

She'd made it to Dallas without spending much of her money. She had no plan at that point, but she definitely wanted to get away from everything she'd ever known. While in Dallas, staying at a homeless shelter that had been much nicer than the Wayfarer's Rest, she'd come up with her plan. She'd heard from some of the other residents at the shelter that Houston was the newest boom town. If she could make it that far, she would have it made. Still, she hadn't expected anything and focused her plan on eventually making it to Mexico.

The road from Dallas to Houston had been a tough one. She'd found a few rides, but most of them turned either scary or just a little too creepy for her. She ended up walking most of the way. The last two months had been the hardest, fighting through the heat of August and September, but she'd kept going and hadn't given up.

She reached Houston about a week before we did and she'd spent most of her money on a cheap hotel room for a few days while looking for work. Of course, she hadn't found a job and was reluctant to spend her last bit of cash on another week in the hotel for a fruitless search for a job. She'd taken her few belongings and slept on the streets for a few days before finally coming across the Wayfarer's Rest shelter just a day before we found it. They'd taken all her possessions as well and she'd been practically alone in the place until we'd arrive just a few hours after the old man in the corner of the room.

She told me all of this in a running narrative. I've left out a lot of the details that either weren't really interesting or would have been damaging to her personally. Things happen on the road and quite a few of them happened to Mallory. I won't go into detail because she was a good person who'd been thrust into very unusual circumstances.

I grew to feel for her and her situation the more she talked. She had a smooth, solid voice and spoke with conviction. It was easy to tell she wasn't making anything up, embellishing anything, or over-dramatizing at all. She obviously didn't really feel sorry for herself, but there was something about the way she stared at the brick wall in front of her. She was reliving all the nightmarish things that had happened to over the previous few years. It seemed that all she wanted was a break, a change, for something to go right in her life.

I was then determined to see that she got out of that place and, at the very least, went with us wherever we went from there.

EIGHT

We'd been sitting there in the garden for over an hour after we'd finished the work. Since our watches had been taken, we had no idea what time it was, but we knew it was getting close to noon. The sun was rising overheard and the heat was bearing down on us. The open sky above us was clear and completely free of clouds. There wouldn't be any rain that day. The shadow that had fallen over a portion of the garden was nearly gone and would fall on us shortly. It was definitely mid-day.

I finally stood up and said, "We have to do something. We need to get out of here."

Linda and Mallory stood up and we began looking for a way to exit the garden. There were no windows in the walls and they were too tall to scale. The only exit seemed to be the door. I tried the handle again. It was still locked.

"I have an idea," Linda said and moved close to me again. "We wait until Steve opens the door and we attack him, take him down. Then we grab his keys and go looking for Johnny and Mitch."

It wasn't much of a plan, but it was a plan. I nodded in agreement and we found our positions beside the door. We waited. I began to think that Steve was not going to come back for us, that he was going to leave us there to rot. We waited for, I would guess, over half an hour.

Finally, we heard the door's lock being manipulated and we tensed, ready to move. The door began to open. I nodded and we made our move.

I led the charge, shoving the door open as hard as I could with my left hand while my right hand was clenched into a fist. Linda was right behind me and Mallory was behind her. I heard a low grunt as I pushed the door open as hard as I could and felt it connect with something or someone behind it. I set my jaw and followed through.

The door had connected with Steve as he'd tried to open it. I'd pushed with enough force to knock him back. He'd staggered a few steps backward and I practically dove on top of him, driving my right fist into his face. I felt and heard something crack as I hit him and he fell backward. My own momentum had been too much, though, and I fell on top of him. But I didn't let up. I swung again, clenched my left hand into a fist, and pummeled the guy. I straddled his chest and let the blows rain down on his face. Linda, meanwhile, stepped up and aimed a swift, hard kick between his legs. His body shivered once and he let out a weak whimper then he fell still. I hit him one more time for good measure then climbed off.

As I stood up, I looked back at Mallory. She had Steve's keys in her hand and she was smiling. It was a great smile.

I nodded and said, "Let's go."

As we started to leave, I had a sudden inspiration. It had been impossible for us to leave the garden and I figured it would be just as impossible for Steve to do the same.

"Hang on" I said and leaned over Steve's prone form.

I hefted him the best I could. He weighed more than I'd expected, but I managed to get him off the floor. I stood up slowly, feeling the stress in my back, and turned toward the door that Mallory had just closed.

"Open the door," I said and took a step toward it.

Mallory quickly pulled the door open. I walked over in staggering, overburdened steps and stopped at the threshold. I took a deep breath and shoved Steve's still limp form through the doorway then quickly closed it. I briefly considered the idea that he was now playing possum and he would suddenly revive at the most inopportune moment, but he remained still. As the door closed, Mallory stepped up with the keys and locked the door.

I took a deep breath, getting my strength back, leaning forward with my hands on my knees. Linda stood a few feet away at the intersection with the main hallway, looking back and forth.

"Which way do we go?" she asked.

Mallory stepped up beside her and pointed to her left.

"That way," she said then nodded in the other direction. "The dining area's that way. We don't want to go back there.

I stood up and walked over. As I moved away, I heard a muffled scream come from the door followed by a weak pounding. I ignored it and kept moving.

With a simple nod to each other, we took off quickly down the narrow hallway. I wasn't quite sure that it was the way we needed to go, but it definitely wasn't the way back into the bowels of the massive building. I grabbed Linda's hand and she ran with me. A glance back showed me that Mallory was just a couple of steps behind Linda.

We ran through the hallways for a while and didn't see another door. The place was a maze of darkened hallways. A few lights scattered around gave us enough illumination to see that there were no doors, but little else. I began to fear that Steve would regain consciousness and come after us, but we finally reached another door.

Linda and I stepped aside, letting Mallory step between us with the keys in her hand. She sorted through them quickly and efficiently until she found the right one. As she looked for the proper key, I kept watch on the hallway. There was no sign of pursuit.

She finally got the door opened and we hurried through. Mallory made sure she had the keys in her hand.

I stopped two steps into the room and could go no farther.

The white tiled room, floors and walls, were lit with flickering fluorescents and revealed the things we really didn't want to see, that we had only suspected in the backs of our minds and had not verbalized.

The two bodies hanging upside down from chains wrapped around their ankles and attached to heavy hooks mounted in the ceiling over what appeared to be an inset bathtub were the bodies of Johnny and Mitch. I stopped and gaped while Linda let out a small gasp and covered her mouth with one hand. Mallory didn't look at them at first. She entered the room quickly, closed the door, and locked before she turned around. When she did, she stifled a scream that came out only as a high-pitched squeal.

We stared for a long moment, making sure the bodies were indeed those of Johnny and Mitch. They were naked and thin streams of dark blood poured from wounds on each neck into the large pool beneath them. We were still standing there when we heard the voice.

"Don't worry," the silky smooth, almost enticing voice said. "You'll join them soon enough."

I looked slowly to my left, toward the opening to a darkened room, and saw motion in the darkness. The silhouette that moved soon stepped into the light and it was Karen, naked once again, but her hands were covered in blood and her large breasts and stomach were spattered with large drops that had started to run along her dark flesh and had congealed.

"And you will all then join us."

"What?" I asked and turned to face her, keeping my body between her and the two girls with me.

Then Karen smiled and I saw the fangs for the first time. They dripped with bloody saliva that fell across her full lips then slowly began to roll from the corners of her mouth.

"I'm sorry," she said. "I had to taste them before I killed them."

She moved closer, her walk more sinuous than before. The look in her dark eyes was enticing and I could feel myself starting to slip into that gaze. Linda's grasp on my arm saved me. She pulled me back a step toward the other door in the room and it broke the trance that Karen had begun. I shook my head to clear the cobwebs and I practically snarled.

"Not going to happen, lady," I said and prepared for her attack.

I shoved Linda back and said through a tightly clenched jaw, keeping my eyes on Karen, "Get out of here. Find the key. Go!"

I could almost sense Linda's nod and she said, "We'll be back."

I didn't look back as Linda and Mallory left. I heard the door close behind them, but my focus was on Karen and her slow, methodical approach. She crouched slightly forward, her hands twisted into claws. Her long fingernails looked like claws and were covered with blood. Her nostrils flared and she lunged at me, swinging with her right hand in a raking sweep. I stepped back out of range, but she kept moving forward. My eyes darted left to right, looking for something to use as a weapon, but I saw nothing.

Karen lunged again, this time with both hands. My reaction time was just a hair slower as I tried to duck under the swing, turned slightly to my right. Her right hand raked across my left shoulder, ripping through the thin fabric of the scrub top. Her nails caught in the material and pulled it with her. I was spun more to my right and I heard the fabric rip. It fell away from my chest as I stepped back to regain my composure.

I looked at Karen again. She licked her lips, looking at me as if I were the steak she'd been waiting on for hours. She moved toward me a little more slowly this time, her eyes locked on me, homing in on her target.

I was no real fighter, but I could hold my own. I'd been in a few scrapes over the years and I hadn't always been the loser. But I'd never before been in a real fight for my life.

Karen moved in and reached for me. I finally had my balance, not just physically but mentally as well. I had expected a confrontation with her, but I hadn't expected to face a vampire. I hadn't believed in their existence and I wasn't really sure that she was indeed a vampire. Still, I wasn't going to let her bite me and find out for sure.

As her arms spread slightly wider, I waded in. I was a little intimidated by her blatant nudity and her near-perfect body, but the thought of her being an undead creature outweighed any attraction I may have felt for her. I started with an uppercut to her chin. I heard her teeth clack together and her head rocked back. She staggered back with the blow and I could tell when I looked at her that she was slightly dazed. I had a slight advantage at that point and I pressed. I pushed forward, swing with careful blows to keep her off-balance. The first few shots went to her jaws, snapping her head to the side with each blow. I followed that with a few body shots, forcing her to bend forward. I finished with a double-hand blow to the back of her skull. She fell to the floor and didn't move.

I took a deep breath and looked around for something to tie her up with. The only things that remotely fit that description were the two lengths of chain holding the bodies of Johnny and Mitch aloft. I shook my head at the thought of trying to get them down, unravel the chains, and bind Karen with them.

I considered rolling Karen over, thinking that I would better be able to determine when she regained consciousness, but the alternative came to mind. If I left her face down on the floor, she would have to lift herself before attacking. If I kept watching, I'd know when she started to move and I could do something about it.

Fortunately, Linda and Mallory returned a few minutes later. They were both dressed in their normal clothes and Linda carried mine in her arms. Mallory still had the building keys in one hand and both sets of eyes grew wide as they saw Karen lying on the floor.

Linda stepped into the room and said, "I got the car key and your clothes. Let's get the hell out of here."

I took a step toward her then stopped and glanced back at Karen.

"Hold on," I said and a small smile crossed my face. "I have an idea."

I took the time to get dressed. Linda and Mallory stood watch over Karen while I removed the remains of the scrubs and put my own clothing back on. As I stood there naked for a moment, both girls took surreptitious glances at me, but I didn't care. I was just happy to have my things back and be almost ready to get out of the madhouse.

NINE

My plan wasn't that much of one, but it was something. If it worked, we'd be safe to leave the place and head home. I told Mallory to get the keys ready and for her to head to the garden door, but not to open it until I got there and gave her the go ahead. She nodded and took off quickly down the hall. I moved closer to Karen and started to roll her over.

Linda stood beside me and asked, "What are you going to do?"

I grabbed Karen around the waist and lifted her as I said, "We're going to plant her in the garden with Steve."

Linda nodded in agreement and helped me get the inert form of Karen over my shoulder.

We took off down the hallway as quickly as I could with the additional weight of Karen.

She was heavier than I'd expected and I couldn't move as quickly as I normally would. Linda walked behind me, watching Karen for signs of movement.

A few minutes later, we reached the door to the garden. Mallory was waiting there with the key in the lock. I moved toward her. The pounding and screaming from beyond it had ceased. I nodded to Mallory to open the door and as the key turned in the lock, Karen moved.

With a rapid thrashing of her limbs, Karen overbalanced me and I fell to the floor with her. We hit the ground together, but she was on top of me. She rolled over and sat on my face for a second and I was sure I would be her first victim.

Linda started toward her and Karen sprang at the slightly smaller girl. The naked woman leapt over my head and tackled Linda, driving her to the concrete floor. Linda landed with a heavy grunt as I scrambled to my feet. I rolled over just in time to see Karen rip the shirt away from Linda's throat and plunge her fangs into the bare flesh.

Blood sprayed and I knew instantly that Karen had hit the carotid artery. There was too much blood. I hesitated just a second and that may have been the deciding factor. I'll never know for sure.

I rushed over and grabbed Karen around the waist. I pulled her up and she held onto Linda for a few seconds. Linda struggled and her thrashing finally helped me pull Karen away from her. Karen began struggling against me, but I wrapped my arms around her waist, clamped my right hand onto my left wrist, and held on as tightly as I could.

I turned around and snarled as I struggled to hold the smooth, slick body against mine. I turned just enough that I could see Mallory and yelled, "Open the door!"

Mallory quickly moved to the door, unlocked it, and started to pull it open as Karen growled, "I will rip you apart."

I didn't respond. I was too busy just maintaining my grip on her. I rushed forward as quickly as I could, which really wasn't that fast, and stopped at the doorway. I let go of Karen and, before she could turn, I shoved her through the doorway into the remaining sunlight in the garden. Mallory was quick to close the door and I had to jump out of the way as she slammed it closed. As I stepped back, I caught a glimpse of something on the ground that looked like it had at one time been human. My first thought was that Steve had been a vampire as well and the sunlight had destroyed him. I heard Karen scream as Mallory turned the key, locking the door. She pulled the key free of the lock and looked at me.

I nodded briefly then turned back to Linda.

She wasn't moving. I hurried over to her and knelt beside her. I brushed a lock of her hair away from her eyes and saw that they were closed. Blood was everywhere. It had soaked through her shirt and spread into a wide pool around her shoulders. The flow from her ruined throat had stopped and that told me that her heart had stopped beating. I remained there a few moments, mourning the loss of yet another friend.

Mallory gave me a few moments then walked over and placed a hand gently on my shoulder. I looked up at her and she said, "I'm sorry, but we need to get out of here. There's nothing we can do for her now."

I nodded slowly, realizing it was the truth. We definitely didn't need to get caught by the authorities or have more vampires show up. I didn't think I could handle another one. I still heard Karen screaming and pounding weakly on the door. I did my best to ignore it and fought my revulsion at touching a recently deceased body as I took the car key from Linda's pocket. Mallory took my arm as I then stood up and we began our quest to escape the Wayfarer's Rest. It took a while to navigate the labyrinthine hallways of the building. There were no lights outside of those few white-walled rooms, but we finally made it back to the room where we'd showered and changed the previous night. I heaved a sigh of relief, knowing more or less where I was. I felt energized and I led Mallory to the front door. She still had the keys and she unlocked the door. We stepped out into the fading sunlight of late afternoon and the scent of fresh air had never smelled so good.

Mallory closed and locked the door once we were outside. I hadn't expected it, but it made sense. She pulled the key from the lock and walked over to me as I stood on the sidewalk at the edge of the street. There was no traffic in that part of the city and I began to think it was just a large abandoned area.

She stopped beside me and asked, "So, what do we do now?"

I hadn't really thought about anything beyond getting out of the building. I really didn't know what to do. Johnny, Mitch, and Linda were dead. There was at least one vampire in the building, possibly two or more, and one old man that we knew nothing about. I closed my eyes and calmed myself down, forcing myself to think logically now that the illogic of encountering vampires had ended.

After a moment, Mallory asked, "Where's your car?"

TEN

We walked the three miles to where we'd left the car. It was still there, parked at the back of an empty parking lot. In the light, I saw that the asphalt was old and cracked with a random assortment of holes ranging from the size of golf balls to the size of beach balls. It was amazing that Johnny had blindly entered that lot and parked at the far end without destroying the car in the process. As we walked across the lot, I started to think that the lot was as abandoned as the rest of the area. It didn't look like a vehicle had entered the lot in a long time.

We reached the car and climbed in. I sat behind the wheel and closed my eyes, offering a brief prayer of thanksgiving for our deliverance from the vampire lair. When I opened my eyes, I started the car and carefully navigated the vehicle out of the lot. Mallory, on my instruction, opened the glove compartment in front of her and pulled out the map we'd used to get to Houston in the first place. It took us half an hour to find a recognizable street and another hour to get back to the interstate. We headed east.

After stopping to fill the tank and get a little food. Our funds were almost gone and I began to think we wouldn't make it to McLain without running out of money, but there wasn't much choice.

Mallory was going home with me. I didn't know what would happen to her once we got there, but it was better than her going back on the road by herself. She had no idea and said she'd worry about that once we got there.

As we drove, I began thinking about what we would tell people and that prompted an unplanned stop. I pulled over at the next exit with a gas station. There was a pay phone there and I wasted a quarter calling the police. I reported the place, telling them that there were three or more bodies in the building, people that had been murdered. I didn't give them a name and hung up before they started asking questions.

Back on the road, Mallory and I began to formulate a plan for what we would say when we reached McLain.

We ditched the car in the woods just across the Mississippi border from Louisiana. It was going to be a long walk, unless we could hitch a ride, but there really wasn't much choice. We started walking and found a series of rides that brought us to the south side of McLain. From there, I found a pay phone and called my parents. In less than half an hour, we were at my house and resting comfortably.

The story we told went like this.

Mitch had been the instigator or the entire thing. He had coerced us into drinking and eventually running away. It was also his idea to go to Houston. We met Mallory there and she was the cause of me being separated from the others. I'd befriended her and the others didn't like that, so they dumped me outside of Houston and took off. That was the last we saw of them.

Mallory had been hitching for a while and helped me get a ride back to McLain. Knowing that there would some issues about the location of Johnny, Mitch, and Linda, she decided to stop here and add her statement to mine, which stated that we had no idea what had happened to the other three. It was firmly believed by everyone.

After a short while, life went back to what it had been. Mallory, an orphan almost of legal age, was entered into the local foster care system, but before she could be assigned to one of the homes in the area my parents agreed for her to stay with us and continue school here until she graduated. That was just fine with me.

I won't say that I didn't think about Linda from time to time. We'd been pretty good friends and that excursion had made me realize that there was the possibility of something more with her. I don't know if we ever would have dated, but the idea had been planted in my mind. Mallory's presence hadn't really changed that during the experience, but I now knew that Linda was dead and Mallory was alive and just across the hall from me. Before the end of the year, we became a couple. In respect of my parents' position, we kept it pretty tame. We didn't do anything inside the house. We were good kids. I guess that time spent in the Wayfarer's Rest had changed me. I just wanted to be a good kid, get through with high school, and move on. By the end of the school year, I was sure that I wanted Mallory to go with me wherever I decided to go.

ELEVEN

There's one more incident that bears mentioning. It happened about a month before graduation, late one night. I was in bed, sound asleep, and a tapping on the window awakened me. It took me a moment, but I finally opened my eyes and rolled over. I froze there, looking at the image in the window. I couldn't believe it.

Johnny and Mitch stood just outside and were peering in at me.

Their faces looked different. Their skin was pale, almost translucent. Their eyes seemed darker. Johnny smiled and I saw a brief glint of fangs. I almost ran out of the room, but Johnny held his hands up and motioned me to the window.

I climbed out of bed and walked over slowly, carefully. I still had no idea what to use against vampires and was a little scared of what might happen. But Johnny and Mitch had been my friends. I hoped that being transformed into vampires hadn't changed them to such an extent that they would attack me without warning.

I stopped at the window and stared at them for a long moment. Mitch then motioned for me to open the window. I weighed my options and decided to just see what happened next.

I opened the window.

They made no move to enter the room or to pull me through it. They stood there for a long moment, just watching me, then Johnny said, "Been a long time, Echo."

"Yeah," I said softly.

"Look," Mitch said. "We just want you to know what happened, that's all. We're not here to do anything to you."

"That's good," I said and they both smiled.

Johnny said, "Here's how it went down. Karen came to us in the night and took us to that room way in the back. She separated us and killed us. She drained out blood, drank some of it, and turned us into this. You killed her and Steve, you know."

I shook my head, "I wasn't sure."

"Yeah," Mitch said. "You really fried 'em. They're nothing but fertilizer now. So, we took over the shelter."

"What about Linda?" I asked weakly.

Johnny smiled, "She's there. Karen didn't quite turn her like she did us, but she got turned. She's there running the shelter while we're here."

"That's good," I nodded. "I hated the thought of her really being dead."

Johnny chuckled, "Good one. But I understand, Echo. You two did what you had to do and you got out of there. I don't think you'll see us again after tonight, unless you end up at a shelter in Houston again."

I smiled weakly, "I don't think that's gonna happen."

Mitch leaned in a little closer and said, "That's the thing. We were friends, but that's over. Humans and vampires can't be friends. Out of respect for that friendship and since you didn't tell the authorities what really happened, we're not gonna bother you. But if you show up in Houston and we see you, if we see you anywhere, you're fair game, understand?"

"Yeah," I said with a curt nod. "I got it. I'm sorry it happened. I wish I could've done something."

Johnny nodded, "Yeah. It's okay, pal. Sorry, but I hope I never see you again."

"Same here."

And they were gone. They walked away and I watched them until they disappeared around the corner. Then I closed the window and went back to bed.

CHATAWA

Chatawa started as something of a horror story about a local legend, but it soon took its own path and became something else. Rather than the monster being the antagonist, it became more of the protagonist. It was a weird situation for me as the characters and story took on lives of their own as I wrote it. It almost feels like I didn't actually write it, just transcribed it.

The community of Chatawa wasn't really a community. It had been at one time, but that was decades in the past when I first moved there with my mother and stepfather in the mid-1980s. There were a few interesting things there, but nothing that really stood out to make it a community. It was a loose collection of houses and institutions, people and places that had little or no connection to each other.

There was the strange church with a home for handicapped children, the type that needed almost constant care. They rarely left their compound and were hardly seen, unless a new one arrived and somehow got out and wandered around the area. It was situated on a large tract of land not far from the state highway that gave access to the area.

It was also just around a sharp curve in the road from the community post office. I guess, in that respect, Chatawa was actually a town. It had its own post office and zip code. That made it official. Of course, I never saw anyone at the post office, not even a vehicle, and with only two ways to get out of the town, going past the post office was required. It was a large, wooden building, panted a sickly green color with a dark slate roof and was situated just a few yards from the rather narrow river that cut through the town. Across from the post office and beside a dirt road, a path really, that led to a few houses up a steep hill, was a constantly running artesian well. I have to admit that I stopped there numerous times. It was the best water in the world, always cold and crystal clear.

On the other side of the river, a long, winding road took you through the wooded landscape of Chatawa. The overhanging trees and sharp drop-offs on one side of the road and steep inclines on the other gave it the air of an old horror movie. I always expected some serial killer or maniac to rush from behind a tree or bush and attack me even though I always traveled the road in a car, never on foot.

The road ended a couple of miles past the river, a T intersection with a large, practically ancient cemetery across from the stop sign beside a small pond on the right side of the road. I'd been in there a couple of times and it was a little eerie, but nothing too frightening. After all, I'd grown up on all the old horror movies and the eighties was perfect for me with a constant slate of rather cheesy horror movies showing all the time.

Turning to the left at that corner took you through a more run-down area. That was where the decrepit trailers and nearly prehistoric houses were located. I only went down that way a couple of times and the things I saw kept me going the other way to the eastern exit, on the other side of the town from the river.

My stepdad owned property to the right of that intersection. Less than a mile down that road another connected to the left and it was down that road that the property, with a rather decent house, was situated. But first, to get there, you had to go past what had at one time been a Catholic school for girls. It had since been closed down and, while still offering weekly services as a Catholic church, the place's primary function was as something of a retirement center for nuns and clergy. I never went into the place and really didn't know much about it. I just saw the entrance to the property every time I went home from school.

Supposedly at one point, years before it became an actual school, the church had opened the facility as an orphanage. I'd even done a little research into it, but I couldn't find out any details other than that it had existed for a period of about ten years, from the summer of 1931 to the spring of 1940. There had only been a couple of articles in the local newspaper that I'd found in the archives of the public library in nearby McComb. It wasn't the county seat, but it was the largest town in the count and actually the seat of commerce.

That orphanage tied into the most predominant legend of Chatawa. I'd heard about it not long after my mother and I had moved to McComb six years before she'd remarried and moved to Chatawa and four years before I returned home after graduating college.

The legend of the Chatawa Monster had been something I'd heard all through high school. I'd always been interested in such things: Bigfoot, the Loch Ness Monster, the Jersey Devil, the Honey Island Swamp Monster, and numerous others. Of course, there was really no actual information recorded on the Chatawa Monster. It was a local legend and had little documentation. It was one of those oral legends, just sort of passed along verbally from generation to generation. And as with all of those, the details altered as the story was retold and generations passed. By the time it got to me, it was something more mythical than it actually was.

The legend as I heard it was that there had been a mutant child born in the woods in the early 1900s and had been raised by a wild woman. The woman had died when the child was still rather young but capable of surviving on his own. Several years later, a teenaged runaway had ended up in the woods of Chatawa and the child, now a wild man, had attacked and raped her. She'd then given birth to a monster. That was the monster that continued to roam the wilds of Chatawa.

I didn't quite believe it. There were too many gaps in logic for it to be real. Like all of those other regional legends, I didn't believe the Chatawa Monster actually existed, nor did I really believe any of the others. I'd never seen any evidence of its existence and I wouldn't believe it until I actually had proof.

I'd just graduated from the University of Southern Mississippi with a degree in Journalism. I wanted to be a writer, but I didn't want to go back to school and teach just yet. The degree in Journalism, with a minor in English, gave me the flexibility to work in news while I started working on the Great American Novel. I'd been writing short stories while in school, when I had some time, and thought it was time to focus on something of greater length.

I was returning home on the day following the graduation ceremony. It was, like all the other graduation ceremonies, long and boring. It wasn't like a high school graduation and there was no brief moment of glory and recognition. That only lasted a few seconds as you hurried across the fairly small stage and took the diploma from the President of the University, shook his hand once, and returned to your seat. My mother had wanted to make a big deal of it, but I assured her that the ceremony wasn't important. The important part was that I'd completed my education and had the paperwork to prove it. She hadn't been in attendance and it hadn't bothered me at all. I'd only gone through the ceremony for her benefit, just so she could feel reassured that I'd actually done it. I was, after all, the first person in our family to actually complete a Bachelor's Degree.

The important thing was that I had a job lined up now that I'd completed the degree. It was with the local newspaper and I would start in just over two weeks. That gave me enough time to return home and finally introduce my mother and stepfather to the love of my life, my fiancé, Jenna Dalton.

I'd met Jenna in a computer class during our sophomore year. It had been one of those simple word processing sort of classes and I felt it would be helpful both in my career as a journalist and eventually as a writer. Jenna had been taking the class as part of her education program. She intended to be a teacher, wanting to teach business related classes, and that had been part of her curriculum. She'd had a few issues with it at first and I'd given her a couple of pointers. From there, we became friends and eventually started dating.

We continued dating and realized it was something more than coincidental that we were on schedule to graduate at the same time.

I'd asked her to marry me a little over a month before graduation, the day after I'd learned that I'd been hired at my hometown newspaper. She'd accepted and began looking for jobs in that area. Up to that point, she'd had no luck, but she had all her paperwork in order and all of her credentials to begin teaching just about anything.

I also hadn't been home in three years. After my first year, I'd returned for the summer and worked a couple of months in fast food. I knew then that I would hate that type of job for the rest of my life. When I returned to school in the fall, I started working with the school newspaper and at near the end of that year I was named as Associate News Editor, meaning that I would effectively be the news editor for the summer. I remained through the summer semester, primarily working on the paper, but taking a few classes as well. I was promoted to Associate Editor at the end of my third year and then to Editor-in-Chief at the beginning of my senior year. The publisher, effectively the head of the Journalism department, wanted me in that top spot, but I had to spend the summer in the associate position while I really learned the ropes of that job.

But that training had helped me get the job in my home town. I was going to be nothing more than a fledgling reporter there, but I'd been prepared for that. I was ready to take on the world. I just didn't know exactly how I would go about that.

With Jenna seated beside me in the decrepit old Toyota that barely held the two of us with some of our belongings and barely made it to the speed limit, we made our way through the narrow roads of Chatawa toward the house my stepfather, Patrick Jameson, had built.

After turning just past the old Catholic school and church, the trees lining the road thinned appreciably and afternoon sunlight finally reached us again. I didn't mind the shadows, but it did feel good to be back in the sun again.

I glanced at Jenna and smiled once again at the thought that I would soon marry her. She was beautiful, with long, golden blond hair, sea green eyes, a body that was just perfect, and the most radiant smile I'd ever seen.

"Almost there," I said and quickly looked back at the road.

She nodded and said, "Good. I'm ready to get out of this car."

We'd only been on the road a little over an hour, but it had already been a long day and we were both rather tired. I did look forward to getting to the house and becoming reacquainted with my old bed.

A few moments later, we arrived. The house was effectively hidden from view behind some thick bushes and a couple of trees. The gravel driveway nearly blended into the dirt around it and, if you didn't know exactly where it was, you would miss it. I knew where it was and it shocked Jenna when I veered off the road seemingly into nothing. She let out a low gasp, but relaxed quickly when she saw the house just beyond the bushes.

The carport on the right side of the house was filled with my mom's dark blue Chevy Cavalier. My stepdad's ancient Chevy II was parked in one of the buildings behind the house. There were quite a few considering that the property had at one time been a working dairy farm. Mr. Pat, as my stepdad was called, had retired several years earlier and sold the cows, but he'd kept the property and most of the machinery. He had two sons that lived nearby and he'd kept the machinery in case one of them decided to go into that business.

I pulled up behind my mom's car, knowing that she wouldn't be leaving until the following morning. It was a Friday afternoon and she always made her weekly grocery shopping trips on Saturday morning. Jenna and I planned to leave about the same time to start looking for a place of our own.

As the car stopped and I shut off the engine, the two dogs that lived there, Sooner and Later, ran up. They weren't exactly my dogs, but I'd more or less been adopted. They were mutts, pure and simple, but they were my mutts. I opened the door and they tried to leap in the car as soon as it was open. They rose up on their hind legs and propped their front legs on my left leg, looking up at me with pitiful eyes. I scratched Sooner, the larger of the two, under the chin while I rubbed Later's head.

After just a moment, they were satisfied and wandered off, just like the always did.

Jenna then felt comfortable getting out of the car. She didn't really have a problem with dogs. She'd just never had one growing up. Her parents wouldn't allow it.

We climbed out of the car and Jenna started around the front as I moved to the back seat and pulled out our two suitcases. As soon as I pulled them out of the car and kicked the door closed, my mom appeared in the door at the side of the house adjoining the carport. She stuck her head out, leaning around the screen door, and smiled.

Evelyn, my mom, was a short woman, barely five feet tall, with average brown hair that she kept cut to about her shoulders, and deep hazel eyes that were almost masked by the glasses she wore constantly, that she'd worn since she'd been a teenager. She'd never been exactly slim, but she'd never been exactly overweight. At the time, as she was just over sixty years old and she'd put on a little weight, giving her a slightly rotund figure.

She smiled as she looked out the door and said, "Well, get on in here. We've already had supper, but there's plenty left."

I smiled and said, "Thanks, mom. Give us a minute."

She nodded once and moved back into the house, the screen door screeching closed behind her. I quickly picked up the suitcases and we headed for the door.

The layout of the house was fairly simple. It was divided roughly into two halves. The front half held the kitchen, dining room, and living room with a small entryway, almost a narrow hallway, separating the living room from the dining room. The back half held three bedrooms and two bathrooms. One of those bathrooms was accessible only from the master bedroom, just off the kitchen. The other one and the remaining two bedrooms were along a narrow hallway that could be accessed only from the entryway. My bedroom was the farthest from the master bedroom.

Just inside the carport door was an opening to the right that led to the basement, the only basement in a home I really knew about in Mississippi. From there, two steps brought us up into the small kitchen. Mom was already at the stove, heating up the food she'd prepared earlier. She only flashed a brief smile as we walked in and made our way to the back.

To appease my mother and stepfather, Jenna and I opted for separate bedrooms. I returned to my old room and we set her up in the adjacent room. It wasn't much, but it was enough for a good night's sleep and to keep my mom happy with Jenna being there.

It didn't take long to get settled in and we joined mom in the kitchen for our dinner. While we ate, after introducing her to Jenna, she explained that Mr. Pat had gone with one of his s to visit another son that lived in Alabama. He was due back the next day and Jenna would meet him before we left.

After dinner, we returned to the back of the house. It was getting late in the afternoon and the sun was finally beginning to go down, meaning it would cool off a bit for the night. The old house had no air conditioning and only a window fan in the bedrooms. I'd grown accustomed to the air conditioning in my apartment near campus and wasn't quite ready for the heat of the summer without it. Hopefully, we would find a decent place fairly quickly and could move in before the true heat of summer set in.

There was also little chance of watching TV there. Chatawa was literally in the middle of nowhere and there was no TV reception without a massive outdoor antenna. There was one at the side of the house, but it was connected to a TV in the living room, one that mom conscripted every evening.

Jenna and I stayed in my room for a while, talking as she looked through the things remaining in the room, things I hadn't taken with me to college. While she looked through the stacks of books and comic books, collection of action figures and associated toys, a few model kits, and a number of magazines, I sat on my bed and told her more about the place and started with the legend of the Chatawa Monsters.

Of course, she didn't believe it either. It was just another one of those local myths, but it hadn't quite grown as out of proportion as some of the others.

A short while later, well after the sun had gone down and the night was as dark as anyone could imagine, mom came in and told us she was going to bed and that she would see us in the morning for breakfast.

She left us alone in my room, seeming to not care if we spent the night together or not. I thought she would've said something to me about that, just to make sure, but she said nothing

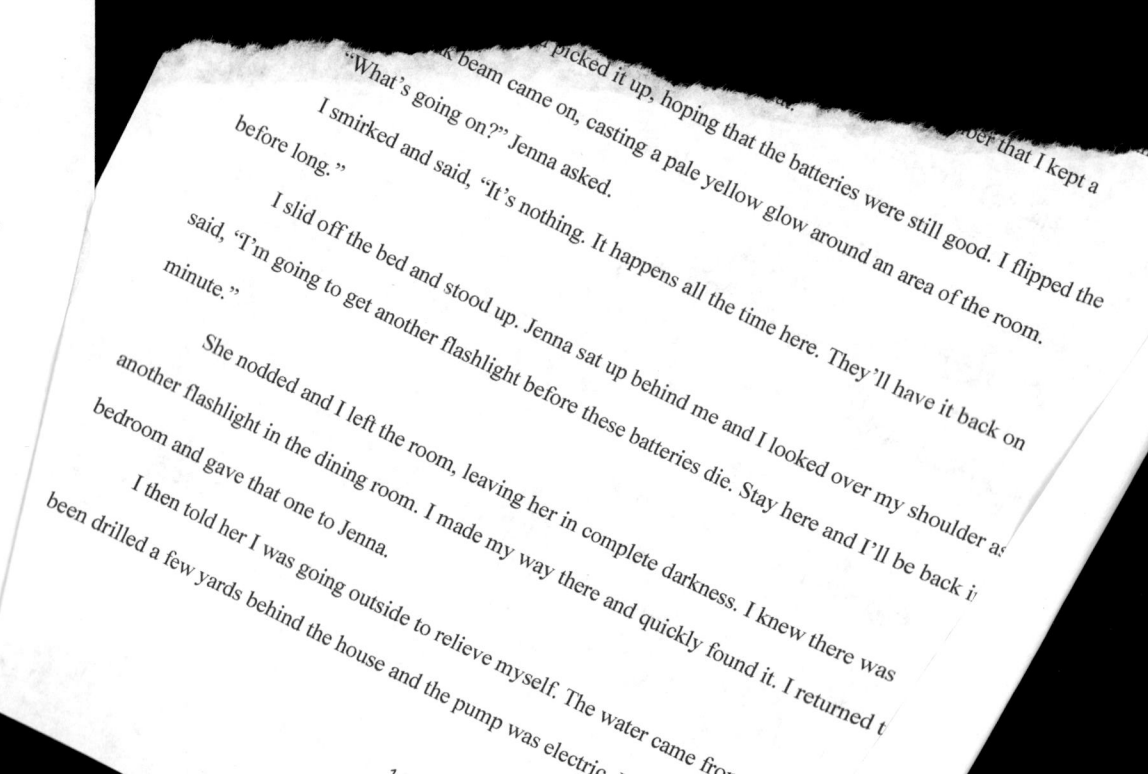

picked it up, hoping that the batteries were still good. I flipped the beam came on, casting a pale yellow glow around an area of the room.

"What's going on?" Jenna asked.

I smirked and said, "It's nothing. It happens all the time here. They'll have it back on before long."

I slid off the bed and stood up. Jenna sat up behind me and I looked over my shoulder as I said, "I'm going to get another flashlight before these batteries die. Stay here and I'll be back in a minute."

She nodded and I left the room, leaving her in complete darkness. I knew there was another flashlight in the dining room. I made my way there and quickly found it. I returned to bedroom and gave that one to Jenna.

I then told her I was going outside to relieve myself. The water came from been drilled a few yards behind the house and the pump was electric